That Something Special

ROBERTA CAVA

That Something Special
Roberta Cava

Published by Cava Consulting
105 / 3 Township Drive,
Burleigh Heads, 4220, Queensland, Australia
info@dealingwithdifficultpeople.info

Discover other titles by Roberta Cava at
www.dealingwithdifficultpeople.info

National Library of Australia
Cataloguing-in-publication data:

ISBN: 97809923579-4-8

BOOKS BY ROBERTA CAVA

Dealing with Difficult People
(22 publishers – in 16 languages)
Dealing with Difficult Situations – at Work and at Home
Dealing with Difficult Spouses and Children
Dealing with Difficult Relatives and In-Laws
Dealing with Domestic Violence and Child Abuse
Dealing with School Bullying
Dealing with Workplace Bullying
What am I going to do with the rest of my life?
Before tying the knot – Questions couples Must ask each other Before they marry!
How Women can advance in business
Survival Skills for Supervisors and Managers
Easy Come – Hard to go – The Art of Hiring, Disciplining and Firing Employees
Human Resources at its best!
Human Resources Policies and Procedures – Australia
Employee Handbook - Australia
Time and Stress – Today's silent killers
Take Command of your Future – Make things Happen
Human Resources Policies and Procedures
Employee Handbook
Belly laughs for All! - Volumes 1-4
Wisdom of the World! - The happy, sad and wise things in life!
That Something Special
Retirement Village Bullies

That Something Special

Chapter one

Joanna sat at the conference table, her brows drawn together in disbelief, her fingers idly playing with a pencil.

'Do you mean to tell me,' she said slowly, raising her eyes to the small group of men and women gathered around the table, 'that Upstage Theatre doesn't perform anything but Shakespeare and Shaw?'

'Well, of course, Miss Marsh,' Mr Bradshaw, a thin, balding man, replied, 'we on the board of directors of Upstage Theatre feel that Sydney deserves one truly serious theatre that specialises in the two greatest playwrights of the English language.'

Joanna looked towards Bill Jacobs, her colleague for support. 'Naturally, Mr. Bradshaw,' she said, 'we all agree that Sydney deserves the best as far as the arts are concerned; however, since Upstage Theatre is having difficulties, would you consider expanding your repertoire a little?'

'Miss Marsh, we are hiring your firm to promote our theatre as it is, not to revamp the philosophy behind it,' Mr. Talman snapped. He was the flip side of Mr. Bradshaw Joanna thought, looking from the thin, dry little man to the other beefy one seated to his left.

'Yes sir, I understand that,' she said, 'now that we know your philosophy, we'll have a better idea of how to promote your theatre. Let's set up a meeting for sometime next week.'

'I have an idea too, Miss Marsh,' Mr. Bradshaw said with a thin-lipped smile. He handed her a small envelope.

'Here are two tickets for tonight's performance of *The Tempest*. You may find you like our theatre's approach to drama. And I'm sorry the creative director couldn't be here today. He handles public relations and would probably have been of more help to you than we were.'

'You were very helpful, Mr. Bradshaw. Thank you for the tickets.' Joanna stood up and shook hands with the board members. 'See you sometime next week.' She said.

Joanna let herself into her downtown Sydney condominium and put her briefcase and bag of groceries in the kitchen. Moving into the lounge room, she flopped down on her light blue sofa with a sigh. It had been a long day.

First there had been the Fenster Draperies. She couldn't understand how a small family business in one of Sydney's many neighbourhoods expected her modern advertising firm to come up with a far-reaching campaign. The company didn't intend to expand or to sell franchises.

She moved into her small bedroom, peeled off her clothes and climbed into the shower. Though she tried to let her mind wander as she smoothed lavender-lotion soap over her body, she found herself reviewing the day's meetings with the

Upstage Theatre board of directors, the Scoop 'n Eat ice cream company's management and the publicity staff from Kennedy Vineyards. Friday always seemed to be her day for meetings with one coming right after the other until she began to fear that she would mention chocolate-chip-and-raisin ice cream to Mr. Fenster and his sons.

She pulled on a flowered cotton housecoat and went into the kitchen. She had about an hour and a half before she would have to leave for the theatre. As she was pulling out salad makings, she felt something furry rub against her ankles.

'All right Alex, dinner for you too.' She told the blue-point Siamese, who seemed to smile as he meowed quietly.

As usual, they ate at the same time. She still wasn't sure why she had named the sleek kitten Alexander the Great. There was no Alexander in her life. In fact, her parents had given Alex to her because they knew she was lonely but was not willing to take what she termed the 'meat-market approach' to male companionship.

Not after Paul, she thought as she dressed. Dear, stupid Paul. She could think about him almost tolerantly now. Of course, that had not been easy a year ago. And she knew that there was still some pain left, because she mentally recoiled every time the memory of their last encounter at the Carlton Hotel crossed her mind.

Seated in the hotel's plush cocktail lounge, Paul had informed her that he had accepted a position in

Madrid and that he expected her to accompany him there. When she pointed out that he had forgotten about her career, which she was not willing to leave on command, he had cast aspersions on her professional abilities and her potential as a wife and mother. Each remark had gone deep into her heart as he sneered at 'Joanna's work,' 'Joanna's stupid love for children's books,' 'Joanna's femininity.' Having barely refrained from pouring her gin and tonic over his head, she had at last walked out, leaving him alone with his accusations and his prestigious job in Spain.

Since then, there had not been anyone significant in her life and she dated little, not wanting to waste her time on men who always seemed to push her beyond her limits.

Joanna looked in the mirror appraisingly. Yes, the dark-green skirt and cream blouse went well with her brown hair and tawny colouring. A little bit of makeup helped accentuate her blue eyes. The light stockings and brown pumps completed the effect.

Alex followed her to the door and meowed, saying quite plainly that he did not like being left alone again. 'It's not fair that a cat can make me feel guilty,' she said to him, picking him up for a hug. 'See you later, Alex.'

'I hope you enjoy the production.' The usher said, handing her a program as she settled down in her seat.

'Thank you. I'm sure I will,' she responded. The board of directors had certainly been generous. These were the best seats in the house; front and centre, with a close-up view of the elaborate sets.

The play began. Although Joanna loved Shakespeare, particularly *The Tempest*, she almost hoped the production would be a flop so that she could suggest that the Upstage Theatre ought to expand its repertoire. Then she would not have to face what seemed the impossible task of creating a campaign for such a limited theatre.

But as scene followed scene and she watched the adventures of Miranda, Prospero, Caliban, Ariel and the rest of Shakespeare's characters, Joanna found that she was charmed. The acting was smooth and professional, the result of a skilled director's work.

The magic of the play had been captured, along with an undercurrent of the emotion she had always sensed in *The Tempest*; sadness. She knew that it was Shakespeare's last play and she had never seen a production that had made its pathos so apparent. The lighting and the sets had also contributed to the effect, she decided.

When the lights went up at the end, Joanna looked around her. Scarcely half the seats were full, but the existing audience was made up of enthusiasts who had clapped unrestrainedly.

After the final curtain call, she went backstage, making her way through a maze of costumes and props. A few members of the cast brushed past her.

'Not bad tonight,' she heard Caliban say to Trinculo, 'but if you drop those lines at the beginning of Act Two again, I don't know what I'll do.'

Joanna arrived at the open area in front of the dressing rooms. A few audience members were arguing with Prospero about the interpretation of his last scene; some of the lesser members of the cast, still in full makeup, were drinking soft drinks and helping themselves to popcorn set out in a bowl on a rickety table. Joanna concluded that the scent pervading this cave-like area was the odour of pancake, the actors' heavy base makeup.

She was no longer sure why she had come backstage and felt out of place, as though in a foreign country. Just as she was ready to leave, someone tapped her on the shoulder. She turned around to see a tall man dressed in jeans and a blue work shirt.

'Can I help you with something?' he asked in a rich baritone voice. Joanna looked up into sea-green eyes and felt something click inside of her that had not clicked in a long time.

'I don't really know,' she said, detesting herself for falling into the helpless-female role. 'I'm going to be doing a project for Upstage Theatre, so I was given some complimentary tickets. I just thought I'd come backstage to get an idea of what it's like after a show.'

'What are you going to be doing for us?' the man inquired, leading her back into the costume room, where the noise level was lower.

'Advertising,' she said.

'Oh.' His body seemed to tense and the curious golden-green eyes became wary.

'My name is Joanna Marsh,' she said, wondering why he had reacted so strangely. *Those eyes are incredible*, she thought. They were an exotic contrast to his dark hair, an unusual reddish-brown, the colour of mahogany. Because his eyes drew most of her attention, the rest of his features barely registered, although she noticed that his nose leaned slightly to the right side of his face.

'I'm Alexander Carlson. I directed this production and I'm full-time creative director for Upstage Theatre.' His eyes were still wary.

'I'm pleased to meet you, Alexander,' she said, extending her hand. She realised that this was the creative director Mr. Bradshaw had mentioned.

His hand, warm and solid, enveloped hers. Their eyes met and she could tell he was speculating about her. 'Would you like a backstage tour, Joanna?' he asked.

'I'd like that very much.'

Alexander Carlson walked her through the wings of the theatre, showing her the lighting controls and the way the props were organised after a performance. 'I'd take you up into the crow's nest, but you should probably be wearing jeans,' he said, indicating the ladder that led up to the platforms several feet above their heads.

They continued their tour. Since the backstage area was rather cramped, she was forced to walk close to Alexander. He was definitely taller than she was, so she decided he must be about six feet one inch tall. His shoulders were broad and he exuded such a masculine presence that she wondered why he had chosen to work behind the scenes instead of onstage. When they returned to the dressing rooms, Joanna asked him, 'Why did you choose to be behind the scenes. I'm sure you'd be a good actor.'

He hesitated, and then asked her, 'Why don't we go for coffee? That way, I can answer your question and we can talk about your project without the place closing up around us.'

'All right,' she replied. She could think of worse things to do than go for coffee with this man with the green eyes.

'I'll get my jacket. Be right back.' He walked away from her, but not before giving her a smile, the first truly friendly one she'd received from him.

The coffee bar they chose was one nearby that Joanna had been to before and liked. The floor was parquet. Plants and ferns rested on the floor or hung from hooks in the ceiling. A classical guitarist sat in one corner playing what sounded like Bach. A few other groups sat sipping their cups of cappuccino coffee around the candlelit tables, but the place retained an air of quiet, relaxed calm.

Once he and Joanna were seated at a table not far from the guitarist, Alexander asked, 'What sort of advertising project do the old boys on the board want you to do this time?' His voice sounded slightly amused and sardonic.

'What do you mean – *this time*?' she asked, sipping her coffee.

'Oh, there have been other campaigns, mainly appealing to the wealthier members of our community that emphasise the classiness of Shakespeare and Shaw.'

'And they haven't worked?' she asked.

'No. You saw the size of the audience tonight. That wouldn't have been bad for a Tuesday night crowd, but no theatre can exist if that's what it gets on a Friday night.'

'Frankly, just because some people are wealthier than others, doesn't mean they're going to prefer Shakespeare and Shaw to motocross races.'

'No, but they can afford to do both'

They paused to applaud the guitarist, who nodded and began to play again, this time a poignant Spanish-sounding melody.

'I know that strategy, believe me,' Joanna said, 'but it doesn't work all the time. For endowments and donations maybe, but not for an audience draw.'

This is starting to feel like another meeting, she thought, disappointed. She had wanted to have an intelligent conversation with this man about his work, about Shakespeare, about all the fun things she liked to talk about, not conduct a business meeting.

'Upstage Theatre is never going to increase its audience unless it performs something other than Shakespeare and Shaw,' Alexander said mater-of-factly, as though this was something he had thought and argued about before. 'I'm not saying we should produce something like Hello Dolly! but there are other serious playwrights besides the two holy S's.'

'I agree with you. I thought they wrote off Eugene O'Neill rather quickly, myself.'

'Then why did you accept the account?' His voice rose.

'Don't get mad at me,' Joanna said. 'I don't choose my accounts, you know. They're doled out by the powers that be. And for your information, I said the very same things you've just said in a meeting today with the venerable Messrs. Bradshaw and Talman. I've been through it all once today and I really don't want to repeat it.'

Joanna took a deep breath. *This is not going at all well,* she thought. *What a shame. He's handsome and bright and I really thought I could have a nice time with him.*

'I'm sorry, Joanna,' he was saying. 'I didn't know that you'd had to deal with them today It's just that we've been fighting about this for years now. I've been with the theatre ever since it opened four years ago and I hate to see what's happening to it. But those overinflated windbags in charge won't consider changing things even a little bit.'

'Then we'll just have to see what happens. As they informed me today, I'm not here to revamp their philosophy, but to promote their theatre. And now,' she said, smiling at him in what she hoped was a winning manner, 'can we talk about something else? You still haven't answered my question about why you chose to be behind the scenes. I'm sure you'd be a good actor.'

'Why are you so sure?' he asked, actually seeming to be curious.

Joanna blushed. *What should she say? Tell him he was a gorgeous hunk of man and should be out there for the whole world to appreciate?* She decided that wasn't a good idea. 'Because you carry yourself with flair – even when you're trying not to trip over cables backstage.'

'Good thing you didn't say that back at the theatre. I would have made you go up into the crow's nest, skirt and all.' Alexander's eyes glowed and Joanna felt the click of attraction again.

'Actually, I did act,' Alexander said, reaching casually across the table to take her hand. Joanna tried to keep her mind on what he was saying. 'But when I left college and got out in the real world, it didn't take long before I was thoroughly disgusted with the backbiting and cutthroat competition you find in the theatre. It got so bad that I didn't care if I got a certain part, because the price I paid for it seemed too high.' He shrugged and grinned lazily.

'So I decided to get some technical experience so I could still be part of the theatre world.'

'It seems such a different world,' Joanna said. 'A whole series of worlds, in fact, since the players spend so much time in one little world, rehearsing a play that evokes still another microcosm.'

Alexander's eyes were so warm that Joanna could feel herself blushing under his gaze. 'I hadn't thought about it in those terms, but you're right.' He said. 'The only problem is when you become unsure of where reality leaves off and the play starts. That mixture of fantasy and reality produces problems in relationships between theatre people. It's hard to realise that the woman in curlers opening the can of tuna fish is the same woman who was Juliet last night.'

Alexander shrugged again, but something in his voice made Joanna think he was speaking from experience. She raised her eyebrows in silent inquiry, but he did not respond.

'I should tell you that I thought the performance tonight was excellent,' she said.

They spoke of Shakespeare's sadness and how the production had brought out that pathos; of other Shakespeare plays; of *Pygmalion* and how they had both known people who strongly influenced someone and then fell in love with their creation; of how the *Devil in Don Juan in Hell* scared them, mainly because they found him intelligent and even likeable.

'People just seem to want to close up around us tonight, don't they?' Alexander said, squeezing her hand before letting it go.

16

Joanna looked around her. The guitarist was putting his instrument in its case and some of the chairs had already been turned upside down on the tabletops; she and Alexander were the only two customers left.

'I guess that's what you'd call nursing a cappuccino,' Alexander commented, looking at his empty cup.

She had left her car at the theatre and he drove her back there in silence. But it was a good silence, Joanna thought, not one she felt she should be trying to fill; instead she had the feeling that she and Alexander were just thinking their own thoughts, along the same lines. She hoped so at least, because her thoughts were of how much she had enjoyed the evening.

'Well, Joanna Marsh, I hope I see you again soon,' he said at her car door. 'I had a great time tonight, especially after we stopped discussing business.'

'So did I,' she said with a smile.

'Maybe we could do it again some time?' he asked.

Joanna's heart began to beat faster. She wanted to see him, but the wariness Paul had caused was suddenly warning her. 'I'd like to,' she answered quietly

Alexander took her in his arms in a big bear hug, a friendly hug that nonetheless made her heart beat even faster than before. She felt wrapped in his warmth. He smelled vaguely of the theatre, of the hot lights and pancake makeup; she liked the smell.

17

He bent his head and kissed her lightly and the smooth pressure was more than pleasant.

'You're nice, Joanna,' he said softly.

'So are you, Alexander.'

'I'll call you sometime soon. You're in the phone book?'

Joana nodded. 'See you later.' She said as she climbed into her car, returning his wave and smile.

Chapter Two

On Monday morning Joanna sat in her office discussing Upstage Theatre with Bill Jacobs. Bill was a few years older than she and had a big-brother attitude towards her. Joanna had no qualms about saying exactly what was on her mind.

'It was a marvellous production, Bill.' She said. 'I've never seen a better one. But I got the impression from the creative director that there's been an ongoing battle with the board about the limited repertoire.'

Bill swivelled in his chair and looked out at the gray-blue skyline. 'We're really in a bind here, Jo,' he said thoughtfully, then glanced at her somewhat sharply. 'Especially if you climb onto the bandwagon. You won't be able to do the job if you decide that the concept of the theatre needs changing. Talman was right: they hired us to promote the theatre as is.'

Turning back to her, he said, 'By the way, who is the creative director for Upstage Theatre?'

'A guy named Alexander Carlson. We had coffee after the performance.' This time it was Joanna who turned her chair and looked out the window at the drab September sky, remembering the warmth of Alexander's hug.

'Ahem, do I detect a conflict of interest?'

'No, you detect cappuccinos in a coffee bar.'

'Uh-huh, sure, Jo. I know you. You're blushing.' He teased.

'Bill, why do I feel that you're playing the part of my guardian angel and supplementary conscience?'

'Because you already seem more involved in this project than in fining a dignified slogan for Scoop 'n Eat Ice Cream.' Bill grinned.

'Well, I guess you'll have to help me out on the Upstage Theatre project.'

Generally Bill was her sounding board for new ideas. Other than acting as a backup at meetings, he rarely worked with her, since their firm preferred individual contribution to teamwork.

'I'll be glad to. But for now,' he said, rising and stretching, 'I have to come up with something snappy for Andy's Autoworks.'

'Sounds just about as inspiring as Fenster's Draperies.' They laughed. 'Why do we always get the winners, Bill?' Joanna asked, shaking her head.

'Because we're still relatively low on the agency totem pole. But if you can come up with something good, I mean really good, for Upstage Theatre, Jo, it'll be great for your career. You've always wanted to work on the artier accounts, haven't you?'

'You mean instead of Fenster's Draperies?' Joanna said with a grin. 'You bet I have. I'd love to work on the Opera Festival promotions and all that nice chewy stuff.'

'Here's your chance, baby. Go for it.' Bill threw her an encouraging smile as he opened the door and left her office.

Joanna sat and stared blankly at the stylised blue, green and white depiction of the Blue Mountains that hung on her wall. *What could she do for Upstage Theatre? What can Upstage Theatre, in the person of Alexander Carlson, do for me?* she thought. The wary part of her mind warned her to stop thinking about him. She had a nice time with the man on Friday night, but he hadn't called her over the weekend. *So don't get your hopes up. And anyway, actors are notoriously unstable. So cut it out right now.*

She forced her mind back to work. What could she do for Upstage Theatre? Without appealing to the wealthy sophisticates she could ... accentuate the funny aspect of Shakespeare ... encourage the board of directors to dedicate the entire spring and summer season to Shakespeare's comedies. Then a phrase popped into her mind: *Shakespeare, Shaw and Something Special.* She could arrange a gala opening for the summer season.

She grabbed her notepad and scrawled, '*Shakespeare, Shaw and Something Special. Gala opening for the summer season. One acts, maybe. Maybe bring in some super British Shakespearean actor.*'

She sighed. *Enough for one morning. On to Fenster's Draperies.*

When Joanna opened the door to her condo that evening, she felt a strange silence. Alexander the Great was not in the living room nor in the dining room. When she walked into the kitchen, she realised what was happening.

'Alexander, you horrible beast!'

Alexander jumped down from the counter, where he had been happily devouring the Cornish game hen that Joanna had put out to defrost for her own supper. He looked at her somewhat guiltily, and then meowed softly in supplication.

'Get that little smirk off your face, you wretched, evil child!' She scooped the cat up and swatted him lightly, then wiped a few remainders of the game hen from his whiskers. Alexander purred and nuzzled her neck endearingly. 'I'm not impressed,' she told him, putting him down.

The phone rang. Answering it, she recognised immediately the resonant baritone voice.

'How are you Joanna? This is Alexander Carlson.'

Her heart jumped a little bit. 'Just fine, Alexander. How are you?'

'Working so hard on the next show and the summer season that if I don't get out of this theatre soon, I may turn into Macbeth and start butchering people.'

'That sounds – volatile,' she answered with a chuckle.

'I was wondering whether you'd like to have dinner with me' Joanna sensed he was smiling;

something clicked inside her again. 'Or do you have other plans?'

'No. No, I'd love to have dinner with you, Alexander.'

'Great. I'll pick you up at seven-thirty or so. That all right?'

'Terrific.'

'See you then. I'm looking forward to it.' His voice had become slightly deeper.

'Me too. 'Bye, Alexander.' She hung up the phone and walked dreamily into the lounge room. She flopped onto the sofa and smiled to herself. Alexander the Great jumped up on her and she hugged him to hr, feeling as well as hearing the heavy purr. The cat looked up at her with huge, adoring blue yes, and burped Cornish game hen.

'Ugh. You're stinky.' She said and brushed him onto the floor.

She went into her bedroom and looked into the closet. Alexander had been casually dressed the last time, but that was right after a performance. For all she knew, he might show up decked out in a cutaway. No, he seemed more the corduroy and sweater type.

She opted for that style, donning a pair of dark-brown cords and a simple cream-coloured lamb's wool sweater. *That way I'll be soft if he wants to cuddle,* she thought.

Once again the wary part of herself screamed at her that actors were unstable and neurotic, affected and stuck on themselves. *All they care about is their career. When he moves along, he'll either force you to go with him or drop you, just as Paul did.'*

'It's just one dinner. He's a nice person. So you stop getting all bent out of shape,' she told herself aloud. Nevertheless, she was more careful than usual about applying a small amount of makeup and she nearly threw her hairbrush across the room because her thick, curly hair just wouldn't turn into shiny, straight tresses.

Alexander the Great had apparently decided that Cornish game hen was a very invigorating sort of nourishment; he was in one of his crazy moods, tearing around the apartment, jumping from chair to chair and diving into the bookcase. When Joanna found a dozen books on the floor and heard the tell-tale teasing growl that meant she was being stalked, she turned toward the sound carefully, knowing that when Alexander was like this, she didn't stand a chance against the long legs that seemed to turn it springs.

She didn't see his blue eyes anywhere as she knelt down to pick up the fallen books. 'Alexander!' She howled as he pounced and she felt cat arms clutching her neck. Standing up, she tried to disengage him. He clung to her shoulders, played with her hair and uttered a frightful mixture of growl and purr.

'You little brat!' she tried to extract his claws without damaging her sweater. Unfortunately, the cat was so perfectly positioned that she could not get enough leverage on any single part of his body to remove him. He sneezed wetly on the back of her neck, having evidently inhaled her hair. 'Alexander, blast it!'

The doorbell rang.

'Oh no!' she groaned. 'I don't believe this.' The doorbell rang again. Joanna realised she must either open the door with her cat attached to her or yell at the animal some more The latter was not feasible, since the Alexander on the other side of the door would become confused.

Joanna grimly opened the door. Alexander Carlson looked at her questioningly; Joanna figured that he could see only two blue-gray cat paws on her shoulders.

'Won't you come in?' she asked, letting him pass in front of her. Alexander looked at her again and she smiled at him weakly. The cat chose that moment to peek through her hair and meow. Then he sneezed. Joanna would have liked nothing better, at that point, than to have sunk through the floor.

The human Alexander came closer to Joanna and lifted up her hair as the cat meowed again, started purring and licked Joanna's ear. When Alexander roared with laughter, Joanna saw the absurdity of the situation and could not help laughing too.

'Welcome to my humble abode,' she said, once they had composed themselves again. 'Now, would you please unhook my animal?'

Still chuckling, Alexander did so carefully. She led him to the lounge room where they sat on the sofa. Alexander the Great had run ahead to settle himself on the arm of the sofa and had become a very dignified example of blue-point Siamese disdain. No matter that the books still lying on the floor gave evidence of the tornado-like side of his personality. Curling his paws beneath his chest, he closed his eyes and ignored them.

'Alexander, I'm sorry about that reception.' Joanna stammered. 'My cat has a lot of personality shall we say.' She felt herself blushing.

'The strange thing was that I could have sworn I heard you say, 'Alexander, blast it,' or something like that, when I came to the door. He looked at her teasingly. 'I was wondering what I'd done wrong.'

'The name of the little devil now posing as a perfect angel is Alexander the Great.'

'Looks as though there's going to be some confusion around here.' His use of the future tense did not go unnoticed by Joanna.

'Uh, could be,' she said noncommittally. She looked up from his brown tweed jacket and saw something questioning in his sea-green eyes.

'I suppose I should have asked earlier whether you had any other involvements,' he said seriously.

She smiled. 'No, I don't.' Heeding Bill's advice from the morning she continued, 'My only commitment is to my job. And since I'm working for Upstage Theatre in a sort of consultant capacity, maybe we ought to stay off the topic of the ad campaign, just so that our board and my management can't accuse either one of us of conflict of interest.' She suggested self-consciously.

She thought, *Wow! Great way to start off an evening – with a sermon.*

'Sorry. I just thought I should get that one out of the way now.'

'No, that's fine, Joanna,' he said smiling. 'You don't have to worry about saying the wrong thing to me. Honesty's rare these days and I appreciate it when I see it.' He stroked her cheek with the back of one hand.

'Hungry?' he asked in a more ordinary tone of voice.

'Starved. What do you have in mind? Oh, by the way, do I need to change? I didn't know what the plan was, so I stayed pretty casual.' She wasn't hinting for a compliment, but he gave her one anyway.

'You look just fine. I was going to tell you that the dress code is always casual at best with me, if that's okay with you. I'm most comfortable that way.'

'Good. So am I.'

They drove to Darling Harbour. On the way he gave her three choices of restaurants. 'There's the Red Chilli Sichuan which is a Chinese restaurant, there's the Umi Suchi and Udon restaurant for Japanese food or the Hurricane's Grill and Steakhouse. Which would you prefer?'

'I'd prefer the last one. I'm in the mood for a steak.' She said.

They were seated underneath a fern in an intimate candlelit booth. 'And if you're as sick of the cooler weather as I am, the plants will make it easier for us to pretend it's summer again.'

'I'm a native. I hardly notice the rain,' she said. 'Although there is a period in September, right about now, when I do get tired of being cold.' She smiled at him. Their eyes met and held and she could feel something melt inside her.

The waitress appeared to take their orders. Joanna chose a veal steak with salad. Alexander ordered a T Bone steak with salad.

'So tell me about Joanna Marsh,' he said, leaning back in his chair. His mahogany-coloured hair nearly matched the shade of his tweed jacket. His eyes shone, illuminated by the candlelight.

He's about the handsomest man I've ever seen, Joanna thought. *And he's even nice – incredible!*

She told him about her growing-up days in West Sydney, her college years and how she had obtained her job with Craft-Marker and Associates. She did not mention Paul.

'Never married?' Alexander asked.

'Nope.' She shook her head and tried to smile contentedly, knowing full well that the single life was beginning to seem empty.

'So you're just a career woman.'

'I'm not *just* anything,' she said, her brow wrinkling. 'Yes, I am involved with my career, but I'd like to have children. Hearth and home sound nice too. And I've still got some good years left.'

'You've still got a lot of good years left,' he said gently. 'And I'm sorry that question came out the way it did. I'm really not sexist in the least.'

'And you, Alexander Carlson, you've never married?' she asked after a short pause.

'Yes, briefly, when I was trying to be an actor in New York. Long, long ago.'

That bothered Joanna a little, but it sounded as though the marriage was over and done with, judging from Alexander's offhand manner. 'No kids?' she asked.

'No. She was an actress – guess she still is – and as far as she was concerned, children were out of the question. Actually, that was just one of the many issues that we couldn't agree on.'

'I had a feeling you were speaking from experience, but I didn't want to pry.'

'Pry anytime you want to. I'm an open book.'

'I can tell, Alexander. It's been a long time since I met a man who's as open as you are.'

'Well it's not going to help anybody if I cover up. It's difficult enough to get to know people as it is. Also, my dear,' he said, tapping his glass against hers, 'I'm not entirely undiscriminating. It's not that people have to earn the right to hear my life story. But there are certain people who will listen and talk and contribute and take, and others who won't. I don't waste my time on those who won't. As a result,' he concluded with a wry, somewhat cynical smile, 'I spend a lot of my time alone.'

'I feel privileged,' Joanna said quietly, studying the ice cubes remaining in her glass. She felt almost absurdly honoured, in fact, that this sensitive man had allowed her to see inside him. As he had said, it certainly wasn't easy to get to know people on any level but the superficial, but he was helping the process along, as though sensing her natural reticence. Even the wary part of her was beginning to relax.

After a delicious dinner, they toyed with the idea of going somewhere else for a nightcap, but since they both had to work the next day, they returned to her condo.

'How old is this building?' Alexander asked, looking at the cornice work in the stairwell.

'1925,' Joanna answered, turning the key in the lock and gesturing for him to follow her. 'It was renovated about five years ago. I've had my condo about nine months now. Would you like a drink?' she asked, taking his jacket. 'I have cognac, Amaretto, white wine and many, many varieties of tea.'

'A cup of tea would be nice.' He stood in the middle of the lounge room floor and looked up. 'The ceilings are good and high. You don't find that any more.'

Joana went into the kitchen and plugged in the kettle. Joining him again, she said, 'I've always had a penchant for old houses. I couldn't live in a shiny new place with no ghosts.'

They sat down on the sofa. Soon Alexander the Great was curled up on her lap. 'In a place like this,

I can wonder about the people who lived here before me.' Alexander was looking at her so directly, that she suddenly felt awkward. She hugged her cat, hiding her face in his silky fur.

'If you'll pardon my saying so, you sound more like a Louisa May Alcott fan than a hard-boiled advertising executive,' he said, not unkindly.

If Paul had said that, Joanna thought, *he would have had that awful sneer on his face.* She remembered Paul's remark about her love of 'the Victorians' and cringed.

'What can I say? I was born late. And,' she added, colouring slightly as she decided to take a chance, 'I am a Louisa May Alcott fan.'

'What other types of books do you read?' he asked with a twinkle.

'You will probably be surprised, but I like suspense books especially those written by Stephen King and Dean Koontz. I like books that take me completely out of my ordinary world into one where I have no idea what will happen next.' Joanna replied. 'I also like children's books and have dabbled at writing some, but have never done anything with the manuscripts.'

Her liking for the children's books of the late nineteenth and early twentieth centuries was something she had become nearly ashamed of. After the breakup with Paul, she had moved her collection of vintage copies of the Anne of Green Gables series to the safety of her bedroom, out of the way of unappreciative visitors.

'I too like to read suspense novels, but I am often too busy to read anything but scripts and e-mail advice from our director.'

'Relating to children's books, don't I remind you of Gilbert?' Alexander asked, referring to the hero of the Anne series.

Joanna's mouth fell open,

'I'm an anachronism, to,' he said with an indulgent smile.

The kettle clicked off. 'What would you like? Plain tea, Earl Grey, peppermint, camomile, apple cinnamon, cocoa, or what?' Joanna asked. 'Come along and choose for yourself.'

'You are well stocked,' he said, inspecting her collection of herbal teas and picking a peppermint bag out of a box.

'I have a girlfriend who says one of the best ways to get to know someone is to look in the fridge an in the kitchen cupboards,' she said. 'Since then, I've hardly dared let her in this room.'

'What has she deduced about you?' he inquired. He sat down on the sofa, his left arm around her shoulders.

'She doesn't know what to think.' Joanna giggled nervously. 'I do my shopping the European way – buy what I need for dinner on the same day, except for meats and frozen foods. So there's usually not much around to go by.'

'Hmm.' Alexander pulled her closer so that her head rested on his shoulder. Joanna willed herself to relax. She wanted to let herself enjoy his touch. But since an eligible male had never been in the condo in this kind of situation, she found it difficult to take Alexander's affection in stride.

'Joanna, why are you so tense?'

She was not surprised that he had noticed. Not much escaped him. He twisted on the couch so that he could look directly at her 'I'm not going to hurt you. And if you're worried about my trying to make a pass – well, I can assure you that I don't try to do that on the first date. So you can relax.'

He added, 'Have you had a bad experience?'

'Yes I have, but I'd rather not talk about it right now.' She looked at him, troubled by what she felt. 'I know that intellectually. It's just not easy for all of me to accept.'

His searching eyes were deep like the sea on a cloudy day. 'You're lovely, both inside and out, Joanna,' he murmured. 'You don't have to worry. I won't rush anything.'

She closed her eyes as he kissed her gently. While the kiss was not without passion, she felt safe and secure, and – cherished. Suddenly her wariness disappeared completely and she wrapped her arms around him, holding him close. His kiss became more passionate. It was Alexander who finally pulled his lips away from hers, taking a deep breath that warmed her cheek when he exhaled.

'You know, there are times when I wish I wasn't so self-restrained,' he breathed, squeezing her hand. 'I think I'd better go before I forget about that sweet speech of mine.' He quickly drained his cup of tea.

Joanna saw him to the door, her mind and senses reeling. Unable to speak, she could only look at his tall form, the strange new fondness she felt for him making her fear that she might dissolve into sentimental tears.

He brushed her lips lightly with his. 'You're delicious,' he said. After a pause, during which Joanna thought she might melt into a puddle at his feet, he continued, 'I'm going to be swamped at the theatre for the next few days, but we don't have a matinee on Saturday. Would you like to go on a picnic?'

'A picnic – when it's still so cool out?' To her disgust, her voice sounded high and shaky.

'Why not? We can always rough it and go to the Blue Mountains or something,' he teased, 'don't worry, I'll take care of the details.'

'Okay. Thanks, Alexander – for everything.' In what she thought was a very daring gesture; she reached up and softly stroked the rough surface of his cheek.

'See you on Saturday,' he whispered, smiling at her.

Chapter Three

On Thursday evening Joanna slammed into her apartment and loudly deposited her sack of groceries on the kitchen counter. Alexander the Great came to greet her with a bouncy meow; she brushed past him and strode into the bedroom. She ripped her work clothes off and crawled into a sweatshirt and the most decrepit pair of Levis she owned.

The phone rang.

'Hello,' she snapped irritably into the receiver.

'Hi, Joanna. I have a break. Want to grab some dinner?' It was Alexander.

She heaved a sigh, unsure whether she could even be nice to him. She'd had a terrible day. The meeting with the board of directors of Upstage Theatre had been anything but successful and all she wanted to do was to glower as she ate a can of soup.'

'Well, I guess not. Sorry, Joanna.' Alexander sounded disappointed.

Before Joanna could remind herself that she wanted to avoid a conflict of interest, she blurted out, 'That board of directors of yours is the most pedantic, backward, downright stupid bunch of toads I've come across in my twenty-six years of life and two years of advertising experience! Everyone's going to think it's my fault that I can't come up with something that will satisfy them. They're making me look incompetent. Alexander, they're incredible! I don't know how Upstage Theatre has managed to survive as long as it has with that bunch of ...'

'Easy! Easy, girl!' Alexander halted her. 'Calm down. What happened?'

'I told you!' she blustered. 'They didn't like anything I came up with and I had the feeling that I was reading Talman's mind. He was so condescending that I knew he was thinking, 'You ridiculous woman. You should be married with five kids at your age, letting a capable man take care of you instead of messing up our campaign.' He implied I'm incompetent. I didn't imagine it.'

'Of course you didn't.' Alexander's voice was reassuring without being patronising and helped Joanna feel better than she had the whole turbulent afternoon. 'Talman is known far and wide for making comments that are so subtly chauvinistic that he can't get into trouble for them.'

Joanna felt contrite. She sat down on the sofa and put her feet up on the coffee table. The cat immediately jumped on her lap. 'I'm sorry I exploded, Alexander. It was the most infuriating meeting I've ever had and it was in the morning, so I had to go through the entire day just steaming mad. I just got home now, so this was the first chance I've had to really let loose. Sorry,' she repeated.

'Listen, why don't I pick up some Chinese food and come over? You can tell me more about it then.'

Joanna was about to agree when she thought of her bag of groceries. 'I just picked up some salad makings. Suppose I take out my aggressions on a can of soup and make a shrimp salad?'

'That's fine. See you in a bit.'

'Great. Alexander, I really am sorry,' Joanna absently stroked Alexander the Great.

'Don't worry, sweetheart. You're talking to someone who knows these people. See you soon.'

After feeding the impatient Alexander the Great, Joanna chopped Mr Talman into pieces several times over while cutting up the green onion for the salad. She was giving the same treatment to the tomato, alias Mr. Bradshaw, when the doorbell rang.

She opened the door and was engulfed in a big bear hug that left her breathless. 'I figured you might need that,' Alexander said. 'I know I needed it.' He was clad in the same blue jeans and work shirt as the night of the performance and that made Joanna feel better, since she hadn't bothered to change.

'I brought this,' he said, taking a bottle of Burgundy out of a paper bag. 'When you've had a bad day, you have to treat yourself to something.'

'Drown the sorrows, eh?' She handed him a corkscrew. 'I'm a great believer in consolation prizes. Did you have a bad day too?' she asked. 'I was so wrapped up in my catharsis that I didn't even ask.'

'I don't think it was quite as bad as yours, because I didn't have to deal with the board.' He poured out two glasses of wine and looked at her from under his dark eyebrows

'When I do have meetings with them, they're as unpleasant as yours was. A guaranteed bad time for all. As creative director for a theatre with a small administrative staff, I do a lot of the same things you do. I have to help create the image of the theatre; I'm partially responsible for the choice of the plays we present and I'm in on the casting too. Also, I'm the closest thing we have to a P.R. man. It's a job with many different duties and although I love it in theory and suffered through long negotiations in order to have an open-ended contract, in practice it can be a royal pain in the neck.'

'Alexander ...' She looked at him while she continued to stir the steaming soup. 'What ideas do you have for the summer season?' Feeling a little sneaky, she did her best to seem innocent.

He raised his eyebrows and said, 'What about your qualms about conflict of interest?'

'Rats, you caught me. Okay. Thanks for the reminder. Believe it or not, I really am a professional. I've just never been in this position before.' She poured the soup into china bowls

'What position is that?'

'Dating someone who's connected with my work.' She balked at what had slipped out of her mouth. What if she were being presumptuous? Two dinners and coffee did not a relationship make.

'What kind of people do you usually date?' Her remark had apparently not offended him.

She dished out the salad, avoiding his eyes. She still had not said anything about Paul and for all Alexander knew, she realised, she could be a woman-about-town type, or a female version of Don Juan. 'I don't date much, actually. That's why I have

Alexander,' she said, attempting to lighten the conversation.

'Which Alexander?' he asked impishly.

She looked at him quickly. 'We are going to have problems around her with those names, aren't we? I meant the Alexander who is at this moment coveting your beef noodle soup.'

Alexander looked down at the cat looking up at him appealingly. He patted the cat's head, and was rewarded with a loud, husky purr. 'He's a nice cat. Yes, indeed,' he cooed. 'And this nice cat isn't even going to get one drop of Alex's soup, is he now. No way, you furry feline fiend.'

'Don't talk to my cat that way, Alexander Carlson!' Joanna scolded him jokingly. 'He ate very well not long ago and if he doesn't behave himself, Mommy's going to lock him in the closet with the vacuum cleaner, which he's terrified of.'

The cat's eyes seemed to widen slightly. He turned and walked away, tail swinging in displeasure.

'How come that worked?' Alexander said, crunching his salad.

'He knows the words vacuum cleaner.'

Alexander looked at her with disbelief. 'Naw. That's impossible.'

'I told you my cat had a personality.'

'No cat has *that* much personality.'

'My cat does.'

After dinner and a couple of glasses of wine, Joanna felt much better. Unfortunately, Alexander had to leave early, reminding her with a kiss of their picnic on Saturday.

'I can't wait. You know, I think you're addictive,' he said, his arms tight around her.

She nuzzled her nose under his chin. 'No, you are. See you Saturday.' She gave him a squeeze and he was gone.

Joanna sat down with a magazine and tried to concentrate on reading. It didn't work. Her thoughts kept drifting to Alexander's green eyes, to his strong, solid body and sweet kisses. He had been genuinely regretful that he had to leave so soon and she found it very nice to know that he liked her company. She felt desirable, more womanly.

Stop it. The wary part of her said. For the first time, the other part of Joanna spoke up loudly, mentally shouting, *Just shut up! I like Alexander. I want to get involved with him.' The wary part of her gave an intellectual shrug, saying in effect, 'Okay, it's not as if I didn't warn you.'*

Saturday turned out to be a fairly clear day for Sydney in late September. Joanna was awake early, her stomach fluttering nervously at the thought of spending a full day with Alexander. *You're acting like a fifteen-year-old on her first date.* She teased herself.

Alexander was due to arrive at ten-thirty. He had told her during one of their now nightly phone calls that he had to be at the theatre at six o'clock for the evening performance, so he wanted to make the most of the day. Her stomach jumped again at the memory of how his voice had deepened slightly as he had said that.

He was becoming very important to her. Too important, too quickly. Probably even more so because she had been so socially inactive since the disaster with Paul. *He's different,* she told herself as she sipped her second cup of coffee that morning. She was willing to admit that Alexander was something special, but she was not yet sure how special he was. Getting to know him was like an adventure, a scary and exciting adventure.

The doorbell rang and she jerked her eyes away from the corner of the dining room that she had been staring at unseeingly.

Alexander smiled at her warmly when she opened the door. Running a hand over the heather-coloured sweater she wore, she said awkwardly, 'You said that the dress code was always casual, so I took your word for it.'

'You look fine,' he said, his voice low, the same voice that made her shiver over the telephone. He bent to kiss her lightly, his lips firm and warm. 'I've never seen you in the daylight before,' he remarked, his cheek against hers.

'Uh-oh, I'm in trouble,' she said, moving away to get her gray jacket from the hall closet.

'No, you aren't,' he said. 'Hi there, Alexander the Great.' He scooped the slender cat up in his arms as Joanna brushed past him. 'Wanna go with us?' Alexander the Great meowed enthusiastically.

41

'Joanna, Alexander wants to come along,' he yelled towards the bathroom, where Joanna was giving her hair one final swipe with the brush.

She smiled at her reflection and called, 'He's really very good about cars. I've taken him on some pretty long trips, and he's never given me any trouble.' She went back into the lounge room, where two pairs of eyes looked at her appealingly.

'If it doesn't bother you, he can come along, Alexander,' Alexander the Great meowed from Alexander's arms. Joanna laughed as she snuggled her head to the cat's and Alexander stroked her hair. The scent of his wool shirt and piny after-shave lotion was intoxicating.

She looked up at Alexander, who said softly, 'This is incredible. Come on, we'd better go.'

They packed their things and Alexander the Great into Alexander's Toyota and set off. The blue sky was pale, dotted with thick white clouds that hinted at more rain in the Blue Mountains. Sydney's skyscrapers disappeared behind them and soon they were nearly in the country.

In the foothills, of the Blue Mountain National Park the gum trees, dense, dark and mysterious – came closer and closer to the roadside. Higher up the steep slope they ran into some rain.

Joanna stroked Alexander .the Great, who sat calmly on her lap. 'There's nothing in the world more beautiful to me than a forest in the rain,' she said musingly

'I remember one time when I was skiing when all of a sudden a pine tree dropped a kilogram of snow on my head!' Alexander added.

'I haven't done that yet, but it's on my bucket list.' She answered contentedly.

Alexander drove to the Wentworth Falls Lake that was hidden amongst the folds of the foothills. Thankfully, the rain had stopped. They spread a plastic tarpaulin and sat down to examine the contents of Alexander's picnic basket and Joanna's paper bag. The cat sniffed his way through the rough grass to the tarp, but soon left to explore

Out of Alexander's basket came corned-beef sandwiches, a jar of olives, potato chips and a bottle of dry white wine. Joanna had packed chocolate-chip cookies, some oranges and several varieties of cheese, as well as a thermos bottle of hot coffee.

Alexander immediately took a couple of cookies and munched, grinning at Joanna as though he half expected her to scold him. He looked, she thought like a naughty twelve-year-old.

'How did you find this place?' Joanna asked, gazing across the glassy lake. 'It's so peaceful.'

'I like to explore, of course. But I grew up on the other side of the mountain,' he said, pointing to the area. 'This lake was nearly in my back yard.'

'So you're a western Sydney boy from way back, huh?' Joanna took a big bite of corned beef, shivering slightly as the breeze puffed across her, ruffling her hair.

'Yep, I was born and raised right here and I graduated from the University of Sydney. The only time I strayed was when I made the terrible decision to go to New York.'

He cut a piece of Camembert cheese, neatly sliced off the rind and offered it to Joanna. 'What about you? I know you're a native, but have you ever lived anywhere else?'

'I've travelled some, but I've never lived anywhere but in Sydney.' Joanne faltered. *Should she mention Paul and Madrid?*

'I had the opportunity to live in Spain at one point,' she said, shrugging, 'but I decided against it.'

She took a sip of wine. 'It would have been as big a mistake for me as it was for you to go to New York.'

'For the same reason?'

Joanna assumed Alexander referred to his failed marriage. 'I think so.'

'Let's drink to you, then,' he said, touching his Styrofoam cup to hers. 'To Joanna, who was smart enough not to go to Spain.'

'But who got hurt all the same,' she surprised herself by saying.

This time Alexander shrugged. 'Just shows you're human. And you've survived.'

They ate in silence, looking out across the lake. Alexander the Great reappeared and Joanna treated him to a few bites of corned beef. The breeze curled around them in soft, cool breaths.

Joanna stood up, 'I'm going to take a little walk,' she said.

'Want some company?' he asked, smiling.

She shook her head. 'No. I want to think.' She started along the shore. She was not upset, but she was affected by the depth their conversations always seemed to reach. They made her feel that her life before Alexander had been simple, yes, but superficial – and bleak. Had she consciously chosen to avoid situations where she would have to discuss anything more serious than politics and the weather? Had she opted somewhere along the line not to allow herself to get involved with anyone new, to limit herself to her parents, a few friends and her cat? She didn't think that she had consciously decided; it had just seemed to happen. No opportunity for real intimacy had come along and it was easy to be isolated.

I didn't do it on purpose, she silently protested.

Alexander came to meet her as she made her way back. 'Are you all right?' he asked.

Joanna nodded smiling weakly. The confusion lessened as she looked into his eyes. She took a step closer to him and he put his arms around her waist. Her arms threaded themselves around his neck. She could feel his slightly rough cheek next to hers and the softness of his hair brushed against her forehead. She felt enveloped in his warmth and it was exactly where she wanted to be.

After what seemed a long time, Alexander put her away from him, running his hands up her arms and across her shoulders until they cupped her face.

'You're very special,' he said huskily.

'So are you.' Joanna raised her face to his. Alexander covered her face with soft little kisses that teased gently.

'That tickles.' Joanna could not help but giggle as his lips found a sensitive spot near her temples.

He stepped away from her with a sigh. 'So much for the mood,' he said.

''I'm sorry. I don't want you to think I'm not romantic. It's just that – well, that tickled.'

To her relief, he chuckled. 'Don't worry. For now, it's just as well that you're ticklish. I must admit it did other things to me and sooner or later you'll be able to see that it didn't just tickle – and what's more, you'll admit it. But for now, I'll let you get away with it.'

His tone of voice was so light that Joanna didn't feel at all uncomfortable with the knowledge that she affected him so deeply. Her gloomy mood had broken, blown away like wisps of cloud.

They spent the rest of the day exploring remote corners of the forest that had been logged long ago, where adolescent gum trees pushed through the splintered remains of the virgin forest. They stopped at the lodge and drank hot chocolate by the window, watching the rain fall again.

As night approached, they returned to Joanna's condo. They deposited the remains of their picnic on the counter and left Alexander the Great to his own devices. Alexander accepted Joanna's offer of a cup of tea and sat own wearily on the sofa.

'What's the matter?' she asked, putting a steaming cup of peppermint tea down on a coaster.'

'It's just that I don't want to go to the theatre tonight. After the performance we're having a meeting about the summer season. The board members won't be there. I assume they'll be getting their beauty sleep – but the cast and most of the management will be.'

He blew on his cup of tea. 'We're very much divided, Joanna.' He paused and looked at her with a certain sadness. 'I don't want to load all of this on you, especially since you're involved, but I really don't see how the theatre can survive the summer season if something doesn't happen to boost ticket sales. I'm going to suggest that we have some sort of gala at the beginning of the season. I know the actors will all be for it, but not the management. They'll fight the idea to the end.'

Joanna looked at him quickly. Was it possible that their minds worked the same way, or had she said something to him about her ideas without being aware of it? 'Alexander,' she said, 'I didn't mention anything to you about a gala, did I?'

'No, why?'

'Because I suggested the very same thing to the board of directors on Thursday when we had that awful meeting. I thought it might be a good idea to open the summer season with a festival of one-act plays and bring in a British Shakespearean actor as a draw. I thought we could also add something special to emphasise a change in the theatre's philosophy – some Harold Pinter or if that's too daring, some

Moliere. I hope you're not writing those guys off too quickly.' She looked at him expectantly, eager for his reaction.

'I don't write them off. They do. Your idea is perfect, of course. But I take it the board didn't think so.'

'No. That's what I was so upset about. A colleague of mine thought it was a great idea too. But the board vetoed it.'

'Blast!' Alexander stood up, shaking his head. 'They're crazy, those guys. Well, I'm going to suggest it anyway. You're right, they'll probably shoot it down, but – what the heck – it's the best idea anybody's had in the history of that theatre.'

Joanna was pleased at his praise of their idea. 'We're pretty sharp, you know that?' he said pulling her to him.

'Great minds think alike,' she said lightly.

'That means that great minds are in the minority these days.' Alexander planted a hard, intense kiss on her lips, leaving her breathless. 'Take care, angel. I'll let you know what happens. Thanks for your company today'

He left quickly. The condo seemed empty without him.

Chapter Four

'Yes?' Joanna pushed down her office intercom button.

'Joanna, you're wanted in Mr. Dobson's office at ten-thirty,' the receptionist said.

Joanna looked at her watch. It was ten-fifteen. 'Okay. Thanks, Marsha.' She clicked off the intercom.

Why would Tom Dobson, the director of her department want to see her? She knew it wasn't because of the wonderful campaign she had created for Fenster's Draperies, which amounted to advertisements stating that their product 'hangs in there.' So what could it be?

He had always been nice enough during their infrequent meetings, but she had been called to his office only twice before, both times at the beginning of her career when she had needed a push in the right direction. Well, luckily, she had only fifteen minutes to get nervous.

Mr. Dobson's large, plush office was furnished in earth tones; the walls were of wood panelling and the entire effect was that of a dark cave, which Joanna found disconcerting. As she entered, she held the file folders containing the information on her accounts tightly in her hands. 'Hello, Mr. Dobson. How are you?' she said.

'Fine, Joanna, just fine. Please sit down,' he said. He was in his mid-forties, the sort of successful businessman Joanna could imagine being totally at ease on the tennis court. His expression was friendly and Joanna allowed herself to relax a little. She smiled and sat down.

'I wanted to have a little talk with you today about the Upstage Theatre project you've been working on,' he said.

'It's been a very interesting campaign, Mr. Dobson.'

'Yes. Yes, I'm sure it is.' He paused. 'Joanna, I'll come right to the point. I got a call from the board of directors yesterday following a meeting the actors and management had Saturday night. They said that the theatre people had ideas nearly identical to the ones you put forward during your meeting last week. Apparently, some of the theatre management got a little hot under the collar and the meeting was not at all pleasant.'

Tom Dobson looked at Joanna over the top of his glasses. Her stomach had begun to churn as the inevitable three-word phrase repeated itself in her mind: conflict of interest.

'Joanna, do you know the creative director for Upstage, Alexander Carlson?' Now she knew for sure what the meeting was to be about and she struggled to remain poised.

'Yes, I met him after the performance of *The Tempest* I saw at Upstage Theatre a couple of weeks ago. Mr. Talman and Mr. Bradshaw gave me complimentary tickets.' She said, mentally kicking herself for sounding so defensive.

'I had coffee after the show with Mr. Carlson in order to get a better idea of the opinions and objectives of the company itself.'

'That's fine. Don't think I'm criticising. I'm impressed that you're concerned and involved with your work. It's just that the board of directors seems to think that both the company and Craft-Marker are ganging up on them to change the theatre's philosophy'

Joanna thought for a minute, trying to decide what sort of approach to take. Should she say that Upstage Theatre wouldn't survive if the philosophy didn't change? Should she explain that she and Alexander had independently come up with the idea of a gala opening to the summer season?

'If you're asking whether there's a conspiracy against the board of directors, the answer is no.' She looked up at the man on the other side of the desk, her face serious. 'When I found out that Alexander intended to mention a gala opening for the summer season at his meeting, I was completely surprised that he had also thought of that idea. There was no conspiracy or any plotting, I assure you.

'As for changing the philosophy of Upstage Theatre, however, I do believe that some small concessions must be made. Last week I finally received the dossiers on the other publicity campaigns that have been used for audience draw and they all seem totally competent. In fact, I can't come up with anything better than what's already been done. You must admit that not even the Melbourne Shakespearean Festival can survive on

Shakespeare alone and that company has as much integrity as any other theatre in the country.' She shrugged. She had probably said too much and she might be taken off the account. But considering her relationship with Alexander, that might be for the best in any event.

For the moment Tom Dobson stared fixedly at some papers in front of him. Then he pulled off his glasses and relaxed back into his chair. 'Joanna, some people would object to any friendship that smacks of conflict of interest. I'm not one of them. I don't see what harm could be done, especially since this isn't a war and we're all supposedly on the same side.'

Joanna felt relief spread through her body. 'Unfortunately,' he continued, 'the board of directors doesn't see it that way. At this point, I'm going to advise you to keep a low profile where your socialising with Alexander Carlson is concerned. Also, I want you to know that you have my full support for your idea of a gala. If need be, I'll intervene. At your next meeting with them, you might want to mention to the board of directors what you said to me about the Melbourne Shakespearean Festival.'

'Unfortunately, I already have,' she said dryly.

'Oh. Well, do what you can. If you need any help, don't hesitate to let me know. I'm a bit of a theatre buff myself,' he said with a smile. 'I've seen several of Upstage Theatre's productions and I thought they were excellent. I'd hate to see the theatre go under.

Joanna stood up, gathering her file folders. 'Thank you very much for your support, Mr. Dobson. I appreciate it. I'll do my best to avoid inciting the board's wrath again, but I can't make any promises. They're not an easy bunch of fellows to get along with.'

'I got that impression myself. Good luck, Joanna.'

Outside the sombre office Joanna let out a deep breath in one huge sigh. She could feel the colour returning to her face and her hands began to warm up. The meeting had gone better than she had expected. But problems still remained. Could she make the board of directors agree with her? If not, what was to be done with the Upstage Theatre? And last, but not least, how would she keep a low profile with Alexander?

That evening she was munching on a spinach salad, her mind half on the newspaper in front of her, when Alexander phoned. 'How'd it go today?' he asked.

'All right,' she said, puzzle. 'Why?'

'Because I got called on the carpet by the board of directors, who said a whole lot of downright nasty things, including that they'd called your boss. I just wanted to make sure you hadn't gotten into trouble.'

'Where are you calling from?' she asked, hearing traffic noises in the background.

'I'm outside the theatre using my mobile phone. I'll explain that later.'

'Do you have time to come over?'

'I've got about forty-five minutes. How's that?'

'Fine. I'd rather talk to you in person than have to shout over the noise.'

'All right. See you.' Joanna hung up the phone. Why had he called her from his mobile phone rather than from the theatre? The board must have given him a line about conflict of interest.

When the doorbell rang, she opened it, a cup of tea in her hand. 'Here. Your favourite, peppermint. Now come on – let's sit down and talk.'

But first Alexander set down the cup of tea and wrapped his arms tightly around her, saying, 'Joanna, this is really getting out of hand.'

Joanna didn't know whether he was referring to their relationship or to the Upstage situation. Probably both. He let her go and they went into the lounge room'

'Okay, so what happened?' Joanna asked, as they sat down n the sofa.

'The meeting Saturday night was absolutely abysmal. Just as I thought, the actors agreed with me, but the management – whew! They said, 'too much money No guarantee that it would work.' Plus we'd have to do something other than Shakespeare and Shaw. So it was out of the question. They wouldn't even consider it. It took a lot of convincing to get them even to agree to talk to the board of directors about it with me.

'Then yesterday the board kept me after the meeting for a private little conference. 'What's this about some chick from Craft-Marker you're seeing?'

they said. Actually, Talman said it, in case you hadn't guessed, since he used the word 'chick.' What makes you think you can get away with joining forces?' they said. They essentially accused me of betraying everything that Upstage Theatre stands for.'

He looked at her gravely 'They also said that we are not to see each other any more, or else.

'Or else what?' she asked.

Alexander put his cheek to hers. It was warm and solid and Joanna loved the feel of it. 'Or else they pull the account from Craft-Marker and I get fired.'

Joanna jerked back, shocked. 'But that's absurd!'

'I know. But that's what they said.'

'Tyrants! What are we going to do?'

'I don't know. Listen; has anybody at Craft-Marker said anything to you?'

'Yeah. The board called Tom Dobson, the head of my department and howled about the whole thing. And Mr Dobson called me in today. But get this, Alexander – he gave me his full support and told me not to worry about any conflict of interest. 'No harm done,' he said. He even said he'd intervene if necessary because he's in favour of the idea of a gala opening too.'

'Interesting.' Alexander smiled. 'We're saved, kiddo.'

Joanna's brows drew together. 'How?'

'Don't you see, Craft-Marker is behind you. So even if the board gets really nasty and kicks me out, we may still have our gala. And when they see how well it goes, they'll take me back. That is, if they actually go so far as to fire me.'

'It's not that simple, Alexander. You've missed a big point. What if they take the account from Craft-Marker?' She still couldn't shake her feeling of shock; it seemed that Alexander was far too sure of himself.

'I doubt they will. They hollered and screamed and protested against all of the past campaigns, but they eventually gave in. Why wouldn't they this time?'

'Because this one challenges the entire *raison d'être.*'

'Too bad. They're going to have to face the fact that if they don't do something pretty soon, they're going to lose the entire theatre. You ought to see the books. By the end of summer we won't be able to pay the property taxes for the theatre, much less any operating costs. They're just going to have to accept it.'

'It is a pretty big gamble.'

Alexander shrugged. 'Eventually they're going to see that they don't have much choice. Don't worry, Joanna. You just keep on doing your job. Try anything you can think of, but don't stop trying to sell the gala idea.'

She nodded, and then shifted her position on the sofa. 'What about the board's other stipulation?'

'What other stipulation?'

Blast! Joanna thought with a sigh. *Well, I certainly can tell what's most important to him.*

'The relationship, Alex,' she said sweetly, trying not to get upset at his single-mindedness.

He turned to look at her and his face cleared, the scowl relaxing into a half smile. 'I'm sorry. My mind was on the theatre end of things, on the gala. As far as our relationship is concerned, we keep on doing whatever we want to do. I wouldn't let my mother choose my friends when I was in high school and I'll be doggoned if I'm going to let Talman and Bradshaw interfere.' He sounded very sure of himself.

'You're pretty stubborn.'

'Absolutely, when it comes to things that are important to me. In this case, the theatre is important, but so are you. Having both at the same time complicates it a bit, but it's worth it to me to stick with both.'

The tone of voice he used reminded her of the first night they had coffee together, when he had given her the backstage tour. He had been fighting for the theatre then and now he was fighting again, both for the theatre and for her.

Although Joanna didn't want Alexander to lose his job, she would have been disappointed if he had bowed down to the board of directors – because she certainly wouldn't have.

'Alexander, I want you to know that from a professional standpoint I'll do everything I can to help save the Upstage Theatre. And from a personal standpoint,' she added, 'I will do everything in my power to help you keep your job ... except stop seeing you.'

He grinned. 'Atta girl, Joanna. I like a woman with spirit.' He patted her on the shoulder and then kissed her softly. 'They don't stand a chance against us. Carlson and Marsh to the rescue.' He raised an eyebrow. 'I betcha we'll make one heck of a good team. In more ways than one.' He looked at his watch. 'Drat. I have to get going.'

He rose slowly. Taking Joanna in his arms, he murmured, 'Thanks for listening. And for caring. You're super.'

'So are you.' She whispered.

His lips came down on hers, hard, reassuring and exciting. When he drew back, he took a deep breath and smiled shakily. 'That ought to keep me going for a while. But just for a while.'

Joanna walked with him to the door. When he had left she found herself thinking about what might happen next. She felt a mixture of eagerness and dread. The Upstage Theatre account had become much more than just a job to her. If Alexander was right and the board did back down, it could pave her way to being allowed to handle the accounts she was really interested in, the ones she believed in. It could also help pave the way to a more intense relationship with Alexander. And she now knew that was what she wanted most of all.

Chapter Five

'I'm absolutely beat.' Alexander's voice was weary, his face pale. There were dark circles under his eyes and his shoulders slumped as if he were carrying a heavy burden.

It was Friday night and they were having dinner at Joanna's place. They had both had a horrendous week. For Joanna there had been a useless meeting with the board of directors of Upstage Theatre, as well as a few frustrating phone calls. She was afraid that the professional image she tried so hard to project was in danger of being destroyed. Of course the situation with Upstage Theatre was responsible for her frazzled nerves, but she had assumed that she could rise above it. She had always worked well under pressure. That she couldn't seem to do so now was demoralising and discouraging.

On September twenty-eighth *The Tempest* closed at Upstage Theatre, nearly two weeks ahead of schedule because of low attendance. The few advance tickets that had been sold had to be refunded, a public admission that the theatre was taking a nose dive. Alexander's temporary directing position ended with the play, so he had more time to devote to being creative director. Unfortunately, that also meant that he had a greater opportunity to become frustrated with the board, disgruntled with the management and altogether snappy and irritable.

Joanna had not witnessed his foul temper, but his accounts of some of the rows sounded formidable.

Although at times he seemed somewhat distracted when he was with her, Alexander had remained loving. Since *The Tempest* had closed they had been together nearly every day from five o'clock on in the evening. She loved it and so did he, it seemed. The more time they spent together, the more comfortable they felt with each other. Alexander was absolutely her best friend.

'We're sure a motley crew,' Joanna replied, shaking her head. 'It's Friday night. We're young. We're vibrant.'

'We're exhausted.' Alexander said conclusively.

Joanna smiled in spite of herself. 'Aw, come on.' She teased in an effort to cheer him up. 'It's not that bad. Let's go out to Jason's Place and go dancing. Your mind may be tired, but your body's not.'

'Ugh. I hate discos,' he remarked flatly. 'Let's just stay home and watch TV. We can make popcorn or something.'

'Blah. You're boring.'

'Too bad, Marsh,' he snapped. Joanna looked at him questioningly. He was serious; his eyes flashed angrily and his jaw line had become hard. 'I've had a monster of a week and you want to go out dancing? Fine. Go ahead. I'll just go on home and sleep' Getting up abruptly, he snatched his hoodie out of the closet, put it on and strode to the door.

60

Joanna followed him and put her hand on his arm. 'Tell me what's going on,' she said gently. He looked so unhappy. The indignation was gone from his eyes, leaving only fatigue and a sort of sadness.

'Upstage Theatre is going to be closed at the end of the summer,' he said without expression. 'We had another meeting today. The board made the announcement. It's supposed to be confidential, but you'll find out about it soon enough.'

'You mean, when they pull the account from Craft-Marker?'

'Yes,' Alexander took his hoodie off.

'Here, give that to me. Go sit down,' she murmured. She joined him at the table.

'You told me that the theatre was in trouble. Are you really that surprised?' she asked.

'No, not really,' he said. 'But there's an interesting twist to it that I think you'll appreciate.' He smiled cynically. 'The main reason Upstage Theatre is going to close is that the financial backers are pulling out now – and why? Because the board of directors will not consent to your idea of a gala and because the board of directors will not consent to an expansion of the repertoire. I don't know whether to laugh or to cry.' His shoulders sagged even more than before.

'Blast it all! I've worked for that theatre for four years now and the board still can't accept facts. This is too much.'

'You know you've done your best, Alexander. It's not your fault.' Joanna's own mind was full of questions, full of conflicting thoughts. 'Why don't the backers just sack this board and put in a new one?'

'That's what they're going to do. The theatre will reopen at the beginning of next year with an entirely new management and a new board of directors.'

'And you mean even with that threat the board still won't budge?'

'I mean the board still wouldn't budge.' He nodded his head slowly. 'They have some idiotic idea that they can take us with them and reopen elsewhere.'

'Good grief.' Joanna looked at her half-eaten plate of pasta. She'd lost her appetite. 'Do you want any more dinner?'

'No. Sorry. It was very good. My appetite just seemed to disappear this afternoon around three o'clock.'

'Alexander, my pet, go turn the TV on. Sit down and relax. I'll make the popcorn.'

She busied herself with washing the dishes. The sound of the television came to her across the sound of running water. She scrubbed away busily, willing herself not to think about the demise of Upstage Theatre. That was one thing about being involved with someone with whom you had a professional relationship, she thought. If you both brought problems home from work with you and they were the same problems, it could get pretty tiring.

Lost in thought, she had not heard Alexander's approach. He put his arms around her from behind, rocking her slowly.

'Thanks for not letting me leave,' he whispered. He kissed her neck; she felt warm and tingly. She dried her hands and turned to face him.

Her arms went around his neck and his rich mahogany-coloured hair blended with her lighter brown. She felt him sigh as though he had allowed himself to drain some of the tension out of his body. She felt protective of him, motherly and comforting.

Silently he kissed her, his lips moving across her face and forehead and coming to rest on her lips

'I'm sorry for the way I acted, Joanna,' he murmured. 'It's been a terribly frustrating period for me, especially today. Then they said that we were supposed to keep this news under our hats, I had a sinking feeling because I'm so used to blurting everything out to you. That's why I was going to leave. I knew that if I stayed, I'd talk.'

'Don't say any more,' Joanna said. 'Kiss me again.'

And he did.

When Joanna was informed on Monday that Upstage Theatre had removed its account from Craft-Marker and Associates, she was the only one who was not surprised. Tom Dobson telephoned her, expressed his regret and reassured her that he did not see the loss of the account as a reflection of Joanna's performance.

'I must admit that I don't understand why they're doing this, Joanna,' he said. 'They're only hurting themselves.'

Joanna smiled. 'The board has its reasons that the mind does not understand.' She quipped.

'Anyway, you did well. So don't worry. I'll talk to you soon,' Tom concluded.

She hung up the phone and gazed out the window. If anything, she felt relieved to be off the account, relieved that she no longer had to worry about her relationship with Alexander as far as their working situation was concerned. As sorry as she was that Upstage Theatre was in trouble, her dominant feelings were positive rather than negative.

Bill Jacobs stopped by to invite her out to lunch. 'A consolation prize, if you will,' he said

It was within walking distance and when she and Bill stepped out of the lobby of their building into the early October air, it was obvious that spring was on its way. Buds poked out of the ends of the recently planted saplings. The branches themselves seemed to strain to reach past the shadows of the high-rise buildings to the nourishing sunlight. Joanna took a deep breath and smiled at Bill.

'Therapeutic, isn't it?' he said as they entered the complex where the restaurant was located.

'It sure is. It makes me realise that the whole world is not necessarily involved in what happens within our building, thank goodness.'

'Craft-Maker can be a fishbowl,' Bill agreed.

They decided to go to a restaurant that specialised in crepes. They were seated between two potted palms at a table that overlooked a park. The outdoor terrace was open, but they decided that it was still a bit too nippy to sit out there. Joanna ordered the onion soup and a salad. Bill, a chicken-and-mushroom crepe smothered in white wine sauce. Joanna had the most delicious French onion soup she had ever tasted.

They chatted about Bill's two children; about his wife, who was trying to decide whether to go back to work; and about his accounts.

'Well, now that we've caught up on all my personal stuff – what about you?' he asked, sipping a glass of white wine.

Joanna chuckled. 'Bill, you know my personal life is not exactly exciting. You've been playing matchmaker for me for ages now and it's never worked. Not one of those blind dates you've come up with for me has panned out. Nor did it work when your little brother from Brisbane just happened to need someone to show him about the city.'

'Yes, but ...' Bill looked sheepish. She knew as well as he did that he had tried to set her up occasionally with men whom he deemed suitable. 'Okay. The fact of the matter is that I thought you would be more upset about Upstage Theatre's withdrawal, especially since you've been seeing the creative director.'

'Ah ha! So that's it! You sneaky devil. I knew there was more to this invitation than met the eye,'

Joanna teased him her eyes sparkling. 'To tell you the truth, Bill, I'm not too upset that Upstage Theatre pulled out. Professionally speaking, they were a pain in the neck to work with. Entirely uncooperative. And you know as well as I do that the best ad agency in the country can do nothing if its client doesn't want something to be done. That's how it was with Upstage Theatre. We were on different sides in a war that was destructive and pointless. Personally, their withdrawal is fine with me too. I've been worried about a possible conflict of interest ever since you started acting as my conscience. It'll be nice not to have to be concerned about that any more.'

'I take it that Mr. Alexander Carlson is rather special,' Bill commented.

Joanna looked up from her soup. 'Yes he is.' She said it with finality

Sticking to safe topics, they finished their lunch and started to go back to the office. But Joanna had the feeling that Bill was not through with the subject of her and Alexander yet. On the corner, he said, 'You're in love with him, aren't you, Joanna?'

Joanna looked up and shook her head. Dear, dear Bill. She would have been insulted if anyone else had asked her such a blunt question, but he wasn't nosy, just concerned.

So what was the correct answer? Was she in love with Alexander? She thought of the mahogany-coloured hair, the green eyes, the solid physique, the kind smile. She was definitely very fond of him. But she was still not sure whether she was in love.

'I don't know,' she answered honestly. 'I'm very fond of Alexander. He's my best friend and I care about him a lot. But you know me – little Miss Cautious. It's too soon for me to be able to say that I'm in love with him.'

He grinned. 'Okay Just don't rule out that possibility, pal.'

'Oh, don't worry, Bill. I won't'

That Something Special

Chapter Six

'Ready to go?' Alexander asked, holding her coat for her.

'Yes.' She smiled at him.

They were going to his place for dinner. Joanna knew he had a house near Sydney, but the distance had always posed a problem, so this would be the first time she would actually see it. It was Saturday evening. They had spent the evening before relaxing from another hard week and Alexander had left early. Now that they had recovered however, it was time to enjoy themselves.

Soon Alexander cut off to the right along a roughly paved road. On both sides of them was meadowland that was just beginning to show the healthy signs of spring. The rains of September had kick-started the change from everything being a dead brown and had allowed the healthy green shoots to peeking through.

A couple of kilometres further on, he turned off again to the right, this time down a dirt road. They went through a rough-hewn gate. A hundred metres or so down the road shone the porch light of a house. As they neared it, Joanna could see that this was not a crude cabin like some she had seen in the Blue Mountains. It was a two-storied house built of brick with cedar siding stained a deep brown. Dormer windows protruded over a porch that ran the full length of the house. As the car came to a stop in front of the house, a collie ran to greet them.

They got out of the car. The collie put his paws up on Alexander's arms and gave his chin a lick. The dog then bounced over to Joanna's side of the car and did the same to her, but since she was shorter than Alexander, the dog was able to swipe his rough tongue the entire length of her face.

Sputtering and wiping her face, Joanna said, 'There, boy. Calm down.' Petting the collie who wriggled happily, she looked towards Alexander. 'What do you call this beast?'

'Max,' he said grinning. 'He likes you. And he likes cats for dinner, so that's why I didn't invite Alexander the Great. Come here, Max, you old puppy.'

Joanna watched the man and his dog gallivanting around the yard, enacting a sort of ritual; Max advanced and Alexander retreated. Alexander clapped his hands and Max pranced. Then as though agreeing the game had ended, Max grabbed a stick in his teeth and retreated to the back of the house.

Joanna looked around her. The house was flanked on the right by several gum trees. On the left was an open meadow dotted with a few other trees. The house seemed protected by the mountains that rose steeply beyond the end of the meadow and surrounded the house on three sides. Nestled in the foothills of the Blue Mountains, it seemed like a stronghold, secure and nurtured.

Joanna shook her head, turning a full three hundred and sixty degrees. 'Alexander, this is wonderful.' She sniffed the soft spring twilight air. Alexander came closer and draped an arm on her shoulders, looking around as well.

'I'm glad you like it,' he said, peering at her intently. 'It's my idea of peace on earth.'

Peace on earth – that's what it was, Joanna realised.

Alexander led her across the front porch and through the carved oak door. Peace. One could feel totally at ease here.

They entered through a small foyer and turned left into a large lounge room. The floors were of shining timber covered by old-fashioned braided throw rugs in browns and shades of orange. It was a man's room. A comfortable-looking brown leather sofa faced a fireplace, which was bordered by tile in varying earth tones and sculpted geometrical designs. A rough-hewn wooden mantel above held a brass hurricane lamp. On either side of the fireplace were easy chairs, each with a brass floor lamp on one side.

Forming a back wall was a long built-in bookshelf that left just enough room for a doorway into what Joanna suspected was a kitchen. Between the windows on the front was a cabinet that held a television and sound system. The total effect of the lounge room was one of warmth and comfort; it was a room where friends could sit and talk, enjoying the warmth of a fire.

'Lovely, just lovely,' Joanna remarked sincerely.

'Let me give you the rest of the tour.'

He led her through the back doorway into a large kitchen that somehow mixed a feeling of modern convenience with an old-style air. The walls were white and the furniture black. It was the sort of room that would seem sunny even on the greyest of days. There was even a pantry, which added to Joanna's impression that this was not a home that had been built by a developer five years earlier. The house had a history.

They went through a cheerful breakfast nook, past a bathroom and out into the dining room, which was finished in chrome and black, again giving it a very modern look. To Joanna's delight, she saw that a window seat was set in each of the large bay windows.

He took her hand as he took her up an open staircase directly opposite the front door. There were four large bedrooms and two bathrooms. One of the bedrooms was being used as a study. In it she saw a complete computer setup, but also an old-fashioned roll-top desk with another brass lamp and an overstuffed armchair near a bookcase.

The second bedroom had a single bed in it and a simple chest of drawers. The third, a white-painted bedroom, however took Joanna's breath away. A huge brass bed sat in the middle of the room on the timber floor. More throw rugs, this time in dark blue-greens, covered the rest of the room. The sloping roof gave the feeling that this room was a house within a house. Smaller window seats with blue-green floral cushions were set in both of the dormer windows. It had a full bathroom with a mirrored door.

'You like it?' Alexander asked, taking her in his arms.

Joanna looked at him incredulously. 'How could anyone not love it? It's a dream! How long have you lived here?'

Alexander gave her a brief squeeze and led her back down the stairs. 'It's an ancestral abode. The fourth bedroom is all storage for my parents' stuff. And the lake we had our picnic at is about five miles thataway,' he said, pointing towards the mountains.

'Where do your parents live?' she asked as they went into the kitchen.

'They moved to the Gold Coast when Dad retired. I should say that they're based there, but they travel around a lot in their camper.'

'Sounds like fun.'

'They like it. They're not the kind of older people who sit on their duffs and dream about how it used to be. They're in their seventies but still in great health. In fact, judging by the last couple of weeks, I'd say they're in better shape than I am.' He smiled. 'Are you hungry?'

'Yes,' she answered Actually, Joanna felt like someone who had suddenly arrived home after years of wandering. She felt an overwhelming warmth spread over her, as though she had come at last to the home of the soul, the place of rest.

'Come back, Joanna,' Alexander teased, waving a hand in front of her eyes.

She laughed. 'Out in space again. Well, what can I do to help?'

'How about making a salad? Everything's in the fridge and I'll show you where the utensils are.'

'How do you like your steak?' he asked.

'I like mine medium rare – how do you like yours?' she asked.

'That's the way I like mine too – not overcooked and just pink. It's amazing how similar we are and how well we get along with each other.'

As they prepared dinner, they laughed and joked and listened to music on the kitchen radio.

'I generally eat in the nook,' Alexander said when the steaks, cooked as desired, were on the plates. 'Instead, let's be formal and eat in the dining room. That way, we'll feel even more relaxed while we eat.'

They both did justice to the juicy meat, the rolls and the salad.

Joanna placed her knife and fork together across her plate and leaned back in her chair. 'Oof! I'm stuffed!'

'What? And you haven't even had dessert yet,' Alexander said, speaking as he speared his last piece of tenderloin.

'Dessert? Where am I going to put it?'

'In the space in your stomach reserved for strawberry cheesecake.'

'Strawberry cheesecake? On second thought, I suppose I can make room.'

'You'd better. It's homemade.'

'*You* made it?'

'What do you think I am, just another pretty face' he asked, laughing.

'Not at all – but even I can't make a good cheesecake,' she said.

'I'll just have to teach you one of these days. It's an ancient family recipe that I cut out of the Sydney Sun last year.'

'Ah ha! One of those. Just like my spaghetti sauce.'

Joanna did manage to find room for a rather hefty portion of cheesecake, which she savoured, all the while warning Alexander that he would have to roll her home.

They stacked the supper dishes in the dishwasher.

'And now,' he said, 'how about a nice cup of tea, luv?'

'Sounds loverly, chum.' She matched his mock British accent. Then, seeing the many varieties of herbal teas on the shelf, she added, 'You're pretty well stocked yourself.'

Planting a kiss on her cheek, he said, 'that's because I didn't know what kind you'd be in the mood for. I seem to stick to peppermint, but I don't think you've had the same kind twice.'

'You mean you got all those just so I'd have a choice?' she asked.

'Nothing's too good for a lady,' he answered with a smile. 'And you're a very special lady. So what if I blew my budget on twenty different kinds of herb teas? I hope you'll come her often enough to take care of every single bag.'

It was a small, silly gesture, but Joanna was touched. The longer she knew Alexander, the more it became clear that he truly cared about her, so much so that he had been thoughtful about the little things that made life special.

'You're a sweetie,' she said, stroking his cheek. 'I really appreciate the effort you took to get them for me.'

'Aw, shucks,' he said, looking genuinely embarrassed.

She paused to look at the different varieties 'After much deliberation, I've decided on the Pelican Punch.' She took a bag from the box and smiling, slipped past Alexander to the kitchen, where the kettle was just beginning to boil.

When they took their tea into the lounge room, Joanna settled into the big leather sofa.

'It's a bit chilly in here. I think I'll light the fire.' Alexander said. He went outside to get some firewood. She heard the back door slam and he returned to the room, his arms full of split logs. Behind him danced the collie, which proceeded to give Joanna another lick full across the face and then stood watching Alexander lay the fire.

Joanna appreciated seeing Alexander in his 'ancestral abode,' as he described it. She had seen how he fitted into the theatre world, but now he also fitted here, out in the country, not too far from the city, but far enough. He seemed stronger here, more independent. All the pieces of the puzzle came together clearly. The fact that he was an actor-turned director-turned-administrator no longer seemed to clash with the image of a younger Alexander roaming the nearby hills.

The wood caught into a healthy blaze. Alexander sat down beside her. Max lay down on the hearth. To Joanna, it made a perfect picture of tranquillity from another, simpler time. Having always felt that she had been born late, she was thankful for the havens of the world where time was not an issue and she could be completely at ease.

Soon, their cups of tea drained, they began to speak of the things people tend to talk about only in the middle of the night – the things that Paul once used too cruelly against her. She had no such fears now. They told each other their wildest dreams, their fears, their philosophies of life. Although both had similar views on many things, there were enough differences of opinion to spark a healthy conversation that was stimulating without being hostile. Alexander lay on the sofa, his head on Joanna's lap and she absently stroked his hair as they talked.

Looking closely at her, he said finally. 'You *do* realise this is very special, don't you?' His fingers traced a line across her face.

She nodded slowly. She felt unbelievably happy and content. Her hand caught his and she pressed it to her lips in a kiss of gratitude. 'This is marvellous.' She was nearly whispering. 'I haven't felt this good in ages. In fact, I don't know when I've ever been as happy as I am right now.'

He pulled her face down and covered it with kisses. Then she felt her lips melt into his. When finally their lips parted, Alexander smiled at her, his face still so close that she could almost feel his eyelashes brush her. He touched her face gently. Softly, he said, 'I love you, Joanna.'

He hugged her close and in that instant, Joanna knew that Bill's suspicion of the day before was true. She *did* love Alexander.

'I love you too,' she heard herself say.

Then his hands were on her face, his palms shaping her, his thumbs rubbing across her lips, then her cheekbones, before his fingers dug into her hair. Her breath caught as he sat up and tipped her head back. He wanted to slam his boy into hers, but held himself in check. It wasn't fear that made her shudder and the sound in her throat as his lips brushed hers was one of hunger.

He'd never needed anyone more than he needed her at that moment. All the misery, all the pain and turmoil surrounding the demise of the theatre had carried him to this point. It all faded at the first hot taste of her. She became pure energy in his arms, pulsing with life. Starving, he dived deeper into her mouth while her heart pounded against his. He stood up bringing her with him. His hands moved down to grip her hips, than her thighs. If it had been possible, he would have pulled her inside him, so great was his need to possess her.

He looked in her eyes and asked the question, 'Are you sure?'

She nodded mutely and kissed him hard.

With an oath, he dragged her with him, up the stairs to the master bedroom with the four poster brass bed.

Impatient, he tugged at her shirt, yanking it over her head and letting it fly. They rammed into a wall as he filled his hands with her breasts. She sighed and reached for him, but could only moan when he bent low and suckled. Fisting her hands in his hair, she held on.

He feasted on her with a wildness, a greed and a violence that staggered her. Her body ached and she offered more.

Joanna could feel and almost hear the primitive drumming beat of her heart just under her skin. She had not known that she could feel such passion for a man. Her hunger could only be sated by a rough and frenzied joining. She wanted him to take her now – as they stood. Then he was pulling her jeans down over her hips and his mouth was roaming lower.

As he slid his tongue over her quivering skin, her nails dug into his shoulders and her body rocked.

She was naked beneath her jeans and his groan of pleasure made her shiver. Alexander could hear her quick breathy gasps as he caught her hips to him. Her legs almost buckled as her body was bombarded by sensation after sensation. Joanna gasped for air, gulping hot air until her system was too full as she fought for release. She cried out, dragging at him towards the bed, unable to bear the tension any longer.

His breath was as ragged as hers as he gasped, 'Look at me.'

She opened her eyes and stared into his. She was trapped there she though, with a flash of panic. She was imprisoned with him. Her lips trembled but there were no words that could describe what she was feeling. She pulled at his shirt, popping the buttons in her rush to feel his flesh against hers. *I'm out of control*, she thought, *but what a wonderful feeling!* as she continued to undress him. Then she trembled as she ran her hands over his damp skin.

He fought to take off her boots as she nibbled little bites along his broad shoulders. Her mouth trembled as she finally lay on top of him. He gripped her hips, lifting her up as she arched her back and took him into her. Her body shuddered as he filled her and as she opened herself she took more of him. She rocked slowly, then faster and still faster driving him past reason as he gripped her hands and watched her ride above him. He wondered at her stamina, his quiet woman was a tiger in bed and he loved her more because of it. As they climaxed, he felt her reach her peak and his own release left him gasping. They both became lifeless, damp bodies as they panted and caught their breath.

As they revived, Alexander was the first to speak, 'I've been fighting that urge since I first met you – have wanted to taste you and make love to you. It has driven me crazy. I hope you're not sorry it happened?'

Joanna looked at him, still groggy from their mating and said, 'I didn't even know it, but my body has been waiting for this to happen too. No I'm not sorry this happened – I feel wonderful!''

'I just realised that we didn't use a condom. I hope it isn't too late to be worried about that.'

'Shortly after I met you I started taking birth control pills, so we don't have to worry about a pregnancy and I know I am clear of any sexual diseases.'

'So am I – free of sexual diseases, that is. I'm glad you're on the pill and a relief that I didn't get you pregnant.'

'The next time we make love, I won't be so rushed – and we can do it properly. I feel like I rushed things too much this time,' Alexander admitted.

'I was just as hot as you were and if you remember, it was me on top – not you!' she laughed.

'Can you stay the night?' he asked.

''No, I'd better not – Alexander the Great has been alone all day and evening. I don't like leaving him too long at a time. Do you mind driving me back home?'

'No problem.'

So Alexander drove her home and dropped her off at her apartment. Alexander the Great pounced on here as soon as she got home scolding her profusely because of her absence. Joanna gave him a treat and topped up his dinner dish and he as soon purring happily.

Chapter Seven

The next day, after feeding her cat and putting on clean jeans and a pullover top, Joanna looked forward to spending the day with Alexander.

'What do you want to do today?' Alexander asked when he picked her up.

'We have the whole day, don't we? No work for either of us.'

Alexander smiled and nodded.

'There are certainly some advantages to your being an administrator rather than a member of the theatre company,' she said.

'There sure are.'

It was a beautiful day, graced with a light blue spring sky dotted with puffy white clouds that never blocked out the sun for more than a few minutes. They had decided to take a long drive and set off, not sure of their destination.

'*We're off to see the Wizard, the wonderful Wizard of Oz,*' Joanna sang as they drove out of Sydney to the south on the Interstate.

'Where are we going to find him?' Alexander asked. 'Should I take this next exit?'

'I really doubt that we'd find him there.' Joanna answered looking to the left at a sprawling shopping mall.

'Well, I guess we'll just have to continue our search.'

At Bondai Beach they stopped for coffee and watched the braver swimmers swim and surfboard in the cool water.

They stopped at Kingsford and Alexander pointed out the University of New South Wales and they drove by a large Australian army depot east of Kingsford.

They continued southward towards Liverpool and Camden. The region became more and more rural and Joanna could feel herself relax.

'You know for someone who's supposedly a city kid, you sure seem to like the countryside,' Alexander said.

Joanna nodded. There was a gray barn ahead. In the field beside the barn, several cattle stood, impassively chewing their cuds and watching the car with little more than polite interest. At the next farm they observed sheep grazing and saw a newborn lamb, so the area was both home to sheep and cattle.

'I do like the country,' she said. 'In fact, I don't like cities, except for the cultural things they have to offer – Upstage Theatre, for example. I bought the condo only because of its age and atmosphere. If I could I'd change the location,'

'To where?'

Joanna shot him a teasing grin. 'To a certain pasture somewhere in the Blue Mountain area.'

'I suppose that could be arranged,' he mused. 'However, zoning laws do not allow additional buildings, so you might have to move into a certain house on the edge of that certain pasture.'

They looked at each other with glances that said, *You know what I'm thinking and I know you know what I'm thinking, so let's not get any more concrete than this. We both know we're remembering last night...*

They stopped at Campbelltown, about 50 kilometres south of Sydney and wandered around the charming town. It was a lovely area.

'Did you know that decades go the Tharawal people drew pictures of cattle with pronounced horns? One can see their rock art at a site called Bull Cave that's not far from here. I checked ahead of time, but they aren't open yet for the summer.

'We haven't found the Wizard of Oz yet,' Joanna said, making her voice sound disappointed.

'No, but we've found a lot of sprites,' Alexander said. 'Some of them escaped from *A Midsummer's Night Dream.*'

'I haven't seen any.'

'You just don't know where to look.' He stopped the car on the shoulder of the road, then got out and came around to open the door for her.

Joanna looked around her. Two feet in front of her was a roadside drainage ditch; beyond that was a low bank that led into the forest. 'So?'

'So, come on.'

'Where?'

'Come on.' Alexander jumped adroitly across the ditch and held his hands out to her. 'I won't let you fall in.'

Joanna jumped. Alexander helped her up the bank and held a tree branch so she could pass beneath his arm into the woods. He followed her and they went on crashing through underbrush and over fallen logs. At a small clearing where the forest floor was bare except for leaves and the occasional fallen log, he stopped. 'Okay,' he said.

'Okay, what?' Joanna asked. She knew he was going to show her where the wee folk lived.

'Look over there.' He pointed to a ferny thicket. 'You've scared them all away. Can't you see them running?'

'Who?'

'The fern sprites. Look, there's only one left.'

Suddenly it seemed to Joanna that she *could* see a wee person poised on the end of a leafy fern frond. 'You mean that little guy over there?' she asked.

'Yep. That's him.

'Well, there's one sitting on your shoulder right now. Can't you feel him blowing on your cheek?' Joanna's check tickled, but perhaps it was a faint breeze. 'He's telling you where to look.'

Joanna looked at Alexander with a smile. 'You're a magical man, Alex,' she murmured. 'There really *are* sprites aren't there?'

'There are all sorts of magical creatures in places like this. And there's still a lot of magic in general left in the world, although most people wouldn't believe it.' He put his arms around her waist and she felt her heart expand as though her soul was reaching out to embrace the world.

'There's magic right here,' she said nestling her head on his shoulder.

Alexander kissed her very gently and Joanna sighed with happiness. Then they retraced their path through the woods to their car.

'As far as fairies are concerned,' Alexander said, as they drove on to Woolongong, 'they have very definite likes and dislikes. Now, no fairy on the face of the earth likes bulldozers.'

'What *do* they like?'

'They like wildflowers and shady glades like that one, where just enough sunlight gets through the trees to keep them warm. They like mysterious places and they're not too fond of us big people. But if they like you, they can lead you to what you're looking for. Why, one time when I was a kid, I nearly got lost on one of those mountains by the house. If it hadn't been for the local sprites, I might never have made it home.'

Joanna was delighted. *Any man who believes in sprites and magic is something special,* she thought. She had hidden her own belief in folklore in her bedroom when she was a child. It had always seemed too impractical and far removed from the corporate life-style. Now she realised that she had buried a large part of herself, a part that was really important to her

'Thank you,' she said.

Alexander gave her a quick, quizzical glance. 'For what?'

'For letting me believe in sprites again.'

'Only special people can see them or hear them, sweetie. I knew you'd be one of them.' He smiled

87

out the window and Joanna felt again that she was about to fly away to play with the wee people out of sheer happiness.

They arrived at Woolongong as the mid-afternoon sun caressed the old Victorian homes on the hillside behind the main street. The town had retained its old-time flavour, most of the buildings having been restored to their original beauty. Alexander pointed out the University of Woolongong. They stopped at a tearoom for coffee and a pastry and then walked along the main street, looking in the windows of antique stores and small arts-and-crafts shops.

'This is such a beautiful town,' Joanna said, gazing at a colourfully painted home. 'I suppose this house should look garish, but it just looks happy.'

'It's funny how houses have their own personalities, isn't it?' Alexander said. 'This one really does look festive, but the one up the street we just saw seemed cold and dark, even though it's bright blue.'

Afterward, they drove around the town and ended up at the beach. At the tip stood a lighthouse, the waves crashing around it. Joanna and Alexander walked hand in hand along the water's edge, letting the waves hypnotise them.

'Do you think it's warm enough to wade a little bit?' she asked.

'Probably not.'

'Too bad. I'll freeze.' Joanna stooped down and pulled off her shoes and socks. She rolled up the legs of her jeans and let a wave break across her bare feet. The water was so cold that it made her feet tingle. They walked on, Joanna up to her ankles when the waves broke, Alexander walking on the wet sand. When they reached the point, the waves were coming all the way up to the stone bulkhead, so he bent down and removed his shoes.

'It's not as cold as I thought it would be,' he said as a blue wave drenched his calves. 'It's nice, in fact.'

'Yeah. Once you get used to it, it's fine. Especially after your feet go numb.

Joanna was a few steps ahead of him and as she turned around to speak, a gust of wind blew her hair across her face. She pulled it back and looked at Alexander thinking how his eyes matched the depths of the water as it would be on a cloudy day.

Later, on the way back to Sydney, Joanna, lost in thought, looked out at the dusky landscape. The relationship with Alexander had become serious far sooner than she had thought it would. And she was glad that the wary part of herself had at last given in and had allowed her to trust Alexander, to love him, to make him a part of her life. She sighed with contentment.

'What was that sigh about?' Alexander asked, as much in tune with her feelings as she was.

Joanna looked at the firm profile, which was now in shadow – the off-centre nose, the generous lips, the strong chin. Unable to resist the urge, she reached up and stroked his cheek, loving the faintly rough feel of it under her fingers.

'The sigh?' she asked softly, running her fingers through the soft hair at the back of his neck, gently massaging the muscles. He nodded and the hard muscles stretched under her fingers. 'I was just thinking how glad I am that I met you, she said simply. 'And how glad I am that we're together and how good I feel in general and how content and at peace I feel.'

Alexander nodded again. 'I've thought the same thing more than once today myself. This may sound trite, but I've never felt this way before. What we have is pretty serious and pretty important, isn't it?' His voice was hesitant.

Now Joanna nodded, feeling suddenly shy. To think that way herself was one thing; to hear it from Alexander was another

'Are you scared?' he asked.

After a short pause, she said, 'No, I'm not.' She knew that was the truth. With anyone else she would probably have been afraid of being hurt, but with Alexander she felt perfectly secure. 'Are you?'

'Yeah. I've got to admit that I am. We're in the early stages of love and it's almost too good to be real. Sooner or later we'll have to come back down to earth and I have a feeling that's going to hurt a little. I'm not looking forward to it.'

The muscles at the back of his neck had tensed, but Joanna continued massaging them. 'Let's not worry about that until we have to, okay?' she said lightly, not wanting the spell to be broken.

'Okay. Agreed.'

And they followed the ribbon of road through farmland, small towns and back to the bright lights of Sydney. As they got closer to her condominium, Alexander reached for her hand and said, 'Last night was so wonderful – I'm still reeling from my feelings. It overwhelms me that we have such compatibility with each other. I have to admit that I thought you would be very shy making love, but you surprised me by being my match.'

Joanna looked shyly at him, 'Do you think I was too forward? A wanton woman?'

'On the contrary, you are so sexy that I'm having problems keeping my hands off you. You turn me on just being near me.'

As they pulled up in front of her condominium, he turned off the ignition and reached for her letting his hands roam over her body.

Joanna felt the need rise in her and she panted the word, 'Inside.'

Alexander felt as randy and impatient as a teenager as he whipped her out of the car. His breathing was already ragged as they stumbled through the hallway to her apartment. As he half carried her to her apartment, they stumbled and buttons popped off his shirt. Joanna laughed out loud. She covered her mouth and said in a softer tone, 'I love having your hands all over me.'

'I'll take care of that. Goddamn it, what's wrong with the door' he exclaimed as he struggled with her keys to open the door.

'Let me do it.' She said and the door flew open. They ended up in a heap on the floor, half in and half out of her apartment. Both were laughing like little children and they shushed each other looking guiltily at the neighbourhood doorways along the hallway.

Joanna worked busily trying to remove his belt.

'Wait. Just let me close the ...' Alexander managed to roll and kick the door shut.

Moonlight came through her lounge room curtains giving enough light for them to see each other. The floor was as hard as concrete, but neither of them noticed as they tore at clothes, rolled and tugging them off. Her shirt caught at her wrists by the cuffs as he lowered his mouth to her left breast. She became a volcano ready to erupt as she vibrated beneath him struggling to release her arms. They finally came free when she wrenched her arms out of the sleeves. She felt flashes of white-hot heat and the longing to couple raced through her system until she thought she would burst.

'Now, now,' she panted.

He plunged, letting his body take over, letting his mind give way to the fury of his need. He felt her tighten beneath him before she let out a cry of triumph.

Pleasure ran through her, flooding her senses and sending her senseless. She wrapped herself around him, so she could take him with her and soon drove him over the edge.

As they lay panting, Joanna felt something brush her hair and realised that Alexander the Great had decided to join their party.

That Something Special

Chapter Eight

Joanna sat at her desk contemplating the day and night before and she blushed so red she was embarrassed. She took a peek around her, but nobody had seen her flustered behaviour. She gazed absently at a new Sydney skyscraper under construction. The crane on top of the building turned slowly and her eyes followed its course.

She was allowing herself a bare ten minutes to daydream unabashedly, to consider all that had happened in the recent weeks. She was about to start work on a new project, a campaign for the Karr Furniture Mart. She had found that it helped her focus on a neutral subject for a while before starting on a new topic. Although her relationship with Alexander was far from what she would term neutral, at least it did not have to do with the super savings on sofas that she had to help the Karrs sell.

October was the mystical month between cool winter and warm spring. It was the month during which she and Alexander had realised they were in love. They were even closer now that they had come to know each other's likes and dislikes and had made passionate love. Every time Joanna thought about it, she felt warm with happiness.

'How would you like to have a party?' Alexander asked.

'I love parties. What do you have in mind?' Joanna asked.

'Well, we could both invite one or two of our friends and have them come to my place for dinner and the evening. What do you think?'

'That sounds like a great idea.' Joanna agreed.

When Joanna went to work the next day, she went into Bill's office and asked whether he and his wife could come.

'Let me talk with Sandy and I'll get right back to you.' He replied.

So, on Saturday, October eighteenth they had invited Bill Jacobs and his wife Sandy to Alexander's house, as well as the production director of Upstage Theatre, Jim Melrose and his friend Brad. The event had been a smashing success. The six people enjoyed themselves in spite of their diverse backgrounds.

After a supper jointly created by Joanna and Alexander, they had read Shakespeare's *Julius Caesar* aloud. When Jim had announced Caesar's assassination, Alexander's dog, who had been sound asleep on the hearth when last observed, suddenly let out a loud howl, startling everyone and making them break into peals of laughter.

Joanna's lips curved into a small smile at the memory as the crane deposited a girder on top of the new building. *That was really fun,* she thought. *We'll have to make it an annual event.*

But then, everything she and Alexander did together seemed to be fun. She thought of their own private celebration of the Rites of Spring that had taken place a little over a week ago. She shook her head, remembering how she had put on a flimsy robe over her jeans and T-shirt and then flit out on the field by Alexander's house, feeling like a true sprite, while Alexander, in jeans and a green sweater had recited pastoral poetry, invoking the gods of old to bless the season of rebirth.

We're silly, she thought. *Definitely silly. But I'm sure of one thing. We're not boring each other.*

She could feel herself blossoming under Alexander's attention, becoming more spontaneous, more willingly sociable than she had been since her college days. People had noticed and commented. Alexander the Great seemed to sense a change in her as well and demanded even more of her attention than usual. Her work was going smoothly. She had been astounded when the Scoop 'n Eat administrators ended up being so pleased with her ideas that they called Tom Dobson to commend her.

'Thanks for your accolades Mr. Dobson. Your comments mean a lot to me.'

'Let's drop the Mr. Dobson. Please call me Tom.'

Joanna blushed a bit, and then answered, 'Okay Tom.'

They finished their meeting and Joanna sighed as she returned to her desk. *That was nice of him.* She thought. *But it's time to get back to work!*

She pulled out a file labelled *Karr Furniture.* It included the company's vital statistics; its size, the sort of market it appealed to, the kind of advertising campaign that its marketing department preferred.

The account had been handled by Craft-Marker before, by a man who had retired last January. Joanna found his notes on previous campaigns very helpful. Sipping her coffee absently, she began to make her own notes.

Time went by and she was so engrossed that she did not realise someone was standing at her office door until he cleared his throat. She looked up quickly to see Tom Dobson leaning against the doorframe in a relaxed manner.'

'Whew,' he exhaled, shaking his head with a grin. 'Such concentration.'

Joanna smiled back. 'Come on in, Tom. To what do I owe this honour?' Tom rarely came to the offices of his underlings; it was more his style to arrange meetings in his own office through his personal assistant.

Chuckling, Tom settled himself in a chair to the right of Joanna's desk. 'Are you free at two o'clock?' he asked.

'Yes – why?'

His eyes sparkled with amusement. 'You're not going to believe this, but we've got a meeting – with the board of directors and members of the management of Upstage Theatre.'

Joanna's jaw dropped. Then she smiled and said wryly, 'You're kidding, aren't you, Tom?'

'No. This is for real.'

'I don't believe it. What can they want now?'

'I don't know a thing, Joanna. Talman called this morning to set up a meeting. He specifically asked that you be there. He also made it sound as though Upstage Theatre would be doing us the tremendous favour of coming back to Craft-Marker. I assume they're re-opening their account with us and that they want you on it.'

'Something is rotten in the state of Denmark,' Joanna quipped. 'This is incredible. I can't wait for two o'clock.'

'Me neither. But I don't think anything is wrong in Denmark or anywhere else, for that matter.' He looked at her with a mockingly reproachful expression. 'Is all the Shakespeare getting to you, Joanna?'

'Not that I know of.'

Tom rose from the chair and Joanna found herself smiling at her supervisor, a man who not long ago had intimidated her. 'See you at two in the conference room next to my office. Okay?'

'Absolutely,' Joanna said.

At five minutes to two Joanna entered the conference room. Venetian blinds at the windows were pulled up to expose the view of drizzly Sydney. She took a seat and glanced through her file on Upstage Theatre one last time.

The only reason for the meeting that she had been able to think of in the hours of speculation that had followed Tom's announcement was that the board of directors had given in. Frightened by the prospect of impending unemployment, they had decided to give a little. Either that or the financial backers had eased up. Joanna couldn't be sure and she couldn't wait to find out.

Tom and Bill came in and sat down. Bill leaned over and said, 'I feel more than a little excited – and curious.'

Tom nodded. 'This one was really unexpected. I hope they'll be on time.'

As though on cue, Tom's personal assistant ushered Mr. Talman, Mr. Bradshaw and various members of the Upstage Theatre managerial team into the conference room.

Joanna's eyes met Alexander's briefly. His gaze was entirely professional, Joanna was glad to see. It would have been embarrassing if her own professional facade had slipped and she'd gazed at him like a love-sick fool.

Tom's personal assistant gave the three Craft-Marker people an encouraging smile and retreated, closing the solid wooden door.

Besides Talman and Bradshaw, there were several other members of the board whom Joanna did not recognise from previous meetings. From Alexander's description, Joanna recognised Randy Fredrickson, the stage manager. All the men around the table looked serious, except for Jim Melrose, the production director, who grinned broadly at Joanna.

Without preamble, Mr. Bradshaw began to speak in his somewhat whiny voice. 'Most of you are aware of the financial difficulties Upstage Theatre has been experiencing. At this point we are facing the distinct possibility that the theatre may close.' Mr. Bradshaw paused, apparently assessing the effect his speech was giving.

'Our financial backers are encouraging us to take whatever steps are necessary to assure the survival of the theatre,' he continued with a dry, humourless chuckle.

Ah ha! Joanna thought. *The gala's on!*

'They agree that the concept of a theatre that performs the greatest playwrights of the English language – Shakespeare and Shaw – has much integrity in theory, but they agree with you, Miss Marsh, that the repertoire of the theatre must be expanded so that the theatre can continue to function and compete with the other fine theatres in our city.

'Therefore, we of the Board of Directors of Upstage Theatre, in conjunction with the theatre's financial backers and the technical management, have determined that the summer season of Upstage Theatre will commence with a gala of single acts selected from the works of Shakespeare and Shaw of course, as well as Osborne, Moliere and possibly Harold Pinter. The exact texts will be chosen by the group present at this meeting.

'We have also contacted John Hamilton of London's National Theatre to see whether he would be available to take the leading role in one of the selections and to direct one of the others.

'Miss Marsh, during one of our earlier meetings, you suggested a slogan for such a gala.' Mr. Bradshaw thumbed through the papers in front of him. 'It was '*Shakespeare, Shaw and Something Special.*' We would like that to be the slogan for this gala.'

Joanna smiled and nodded. She did not want Mr. Bradshaw or Mr. Talman to think she felt smug because of this turn of events, so she tried to keep her smile modest, though she felt like cheering out of sheer jubilance. Mr. Bradshaw was eating crow with a lot of style and she found herself admiring the thin little man.

'The dates for the gala have been set for the second and third weekends in January, so we have much to do in a very short time. We apologise for this, but under the circumstances the delay in making a decision was unavoidable. Miss Marsh, the account will be yours. Or should I have left that to you to announce Mr. Dobson?' Mr. Bradshaw asked nearly deferentially.

'No. Please continue,' Tom said.

'At any rate, Miss March, we trust that you are acquainted with the customary procedures associated with an event of this sort and we leave all the publicity and promotional needs in your hands. Mr. Dobson has assured us that he will be available to help you in any way necessary and of course Alexander Carlson, our creative director, whom I believe you already know, will also be at your disposal, particularly during the final stages of the campaign.'

Bless him, Joanna thought. *He wasn't even malicious about that!*

'So,' he concluded with a nearly gentle smile, 'are there any questions?'

'Just in case it wasn't entirely clear,' Mr Talman boomed, 'I'd like to emphasise that Miss Marsh's counterpart at Upstage Theatre will be Mr. Carlson. He will be your main contact at the theatre and you can coordinate the press releases and so forth through him.' He passed Joanna a list containing the names and titles of the entire management staff of Upstage Theatre. 'And if you need any additional assistance, feel free to call anyone listed here.'

'Also,' Mr. Bradshaw said, 'we'll be having daily meetings at the theatre, which you're welcome to attend, Miss Marsh, as well as weekly meetings here. Since the board considers this entire venture something of a risk, we want to keep very close track of its progress.' He nervously checked the knot of his tie and looked fixedly at the centre of the table.

'You don't have a thing to worry about, gentlemen,' Tom said, smiling at Joanna. 'Miss Marsh is very competent and between Craft-Marker and your own talented company, I'm sure the gala will be a total success. Now, where do we begin?'

Two and a half hours passed as they brainstormed. They sketched out press releases, discussed newspaper and radio advertisements and generally tried to plan the campaign for the gala that was itself still in the first stages of planning.

Neither the program nor the cast were yet firm and when the subject came up, it was obvious why:

The board still preferred a full program of Shakespeare and Shaw, while Jim Melrose was prepared to put on *Oh, Calcutta!*. Alexander meanwhile, was trying to maintain a balance and was pushing for single acts from plays by Shakespeare and Shaw, plus Moliere and Osborne.

When at last they emerged from the conference room and went their own ways, Joanna was exhausted and intellectually drained. Yet as she walked towards her office she felt deeply satisfied. She sat down at her desk and looked at the notes she had taken. *What a job!* She thought with a sigh. *The next two months are going to be insane.*

'Joanna?'

She looked up and saw Alexander in the doorway. She smiled; the first spontaneous smile she had given him the entire afternoon. He looked as tired as she felt.

'Hi,' she said gently. 'How're you doing?'

He crossed the room, his long strides taking him to the same chair Tom had sat in earlier in the day. 'Pooped,' he replied. 'And starved. Want to get some dinner?'

She had been so busy that she hadn't noticed it was already past her dinnertime. 'Sounds good to me.' She got her jacket from the hook on the back of her door and stretched. 'What a long meeting that was!'

Alexander nodded. 'No kidding.' They walked in silence and it was an unusual silence although

Joanna could not have said why. At the lift, they saw Jim Melrose waiting for them.

'Hi kids. Where are you off to?' Jim was a short man in his late forties. A bundle of energy, he instilled that quality in everything he did as production director. He inspired the company to heights they might not otherwise have attained, making the most dark and ominous of Shakespeare's tragedies quiver with dramatic tension.

'Off to get nourishment for the body.' Alexander said, 'and solace, we hope, for the soul.'

'Mind if I come along?' Jim asked.

Joanna looked at Alexander, willing him to refuse. She needed to be alone with him to recover from the marathon meeting.

'Sure. Fine with me. Okay with you Joanna?'

Joanna forced a nod.

'Great! Let's go Chinese,' Jim said. 'It's on me.'

They made the trip to a small Chinese restaurant in silence. Seated at the dimly lit table, the strains of dissonant Oriental music flowing around them, they settled on a meal of Chow Mein, prawns, almond-fried chicken and stir-fried pea pods. Over her first cup of tea, Joanna looked at Alexander. He still seemed too quiet. Something strange lurked in his eyes.

'Listen, you two, I have something to discuss with you,' Jim said, some of his bounciness gone.

Alexander sighed, 'Jim, you're a good pal, but you don't know when to quit. Can't we wait?'

'Afraid not. And it's not something I could have brought up during the meeting.'

Joanna felt dread rising in her.

'It's about you two,' Jim went on. 'And it's like this. It's pretty clear that you two are an item. I mean, I know it from the party we had. But even if I didn't know it, I would have guessed.'

'So?' Alexander replied.

'Well, you realise that during the gala I'm going to have to deal with a bunch of temperamental actors and actresses. Take it from me; lovers' quarrels can really screw up a production. Now, I can handle actors. All you have to do is give them an ego boost every so often. But you two are different. If you fought, the press releases wouldn't go out, the programs wouldn't get printed and we wouldn't have a gala. I wouldn't know what to do. So just break it off now for the next couple of months and spare everybody a lot of pain.'

'But ...' Joanna protested.

'No buts, Joanna.' Jim's voice was firm. 'The board and I actually agree about something for once. Whether you guys have a good relationship now is not the point. Nerves get frazzled and I can guarantee you that, involved or not, you'll have had some memorable rows by the time the gala starts. So be nice and take a two-month vacation from each other, just for old Jim's sake, okay?'

'He's right, Jo,' Alexander said, too quickly. 'I know the theatre and Jim is right. We'll have to do it the way he says.'

106

Joanna looked at Alexander, trying to read his eyes. They were completely expressionless, as though he had already decided to put Jim's instructions into effect.

'All right,' she said with a shrug. 'I guess I don't have any choice, do I' She sent Alexander a glance that said, *I'll take this up with you later.*

The meal, which would have been delicious under other circumstances, was tasteless to Joanna. She ate in silence while Jim and Alexander argued about repertoire. She remained silent during the ride back to the theatre and only waved when Jim climbed out of Alexander's car saying, 'Ciao! And thanks again, friends'

Sydney's bright streets passed by as Alexander drove her back to Craft-Marker. Stoplights were a blur of green, amber and red; laughing groups jaywalked from one nightclub to another. Joanna still remained silent, trying to understand that this was the last time she would see Alexander socially for two months.

'Joanna?' Alexanders vice broke into her thoughts as they reached the parking lot.

She looked over at him, unable to speak. He switched off the engine.

'It'll be all right, I'm sure of it' His warm hand covered hers. 'It's only until January.' He looked guilty, but his eyes pleaded for her to understand. Something in her own expression must have shown how she felt, because a harshness stole across his features. 'You don't think we'll make it, do you? He said.

She shrugged, her feeling of desolation deepening until she thought she would burst into tears. She forced the tears back. 'Do you?' Her voice was sharper than she intended. 'Do you want us to?'

'You can determine certain patterns from past experience,' he said acidly. 'These past couple of months have been marvellous and just because we won't be involved for a while doesn't mean it's going to kill all the feelings we had for each other.'

'How come you're using the past tense, Carlson? Or may I still call you Alexander?'

'Joanna, you're making a mountain out of a mole-hill. This isn't that big a deal.'

Again she shrugged. 'Whatever you say, Mr. Carlson. But the way I see it, you just accepted what Jim said too easily. Something tells me you're scared of what we've come to mean to each other. Well, I'm bushed. I guess I'll be seeing you around. Good night.' Without another word, she was out of his car and hurrying to her own.

The honk of his horn went unacknowledged, but the state of his mind was evident as he tore out of the parking lot with a screech of tires.

Joanna drove home, feeling numb. Automatically, she fed Alexander the Great and undressed. She made herself a cup of tea and settled down on the sofa. Her cat came to join her; hungry for the attention he had recently been denied.

Stroking the purring, nuzzling ball of fur, she murmured, 'At least you love me, Alexander.'

She could not help feeling betrayed. *He gave in, just like that,* she thought, *How could he? He didn't even fight.* She remembered what he had said on the way back from their day trip. *Maybe all he wanted was to have an affair with me, and now that we have had sex, he wants no part of me.* Then she had another thought. *Maybe he's scared. Now that the first sweet joy of falling in love is over, he's scared and running like a rabbit.*

When she finally went to bed, it was with the thump of reality that Alexander didn't really love her as he'd said he did. She felt that she had been betrayed and realised that she had definitely come back down to earth – only to find that she was all alone - again.

That Something Special

Chapter Nine

All through November the weather heated up. Joanna watched as all the flowers bloomed. The weather was so hot that whenever she was outside in the sun for more than ten minutes, she found herself sweating and miserable. She was thankful that she had air conditioning in her home and at the office. However, she had her clients to deal with and some did not have air conditioning and she was miserable.

Joanna was distraught and missed Alexander, but not in the way she had missed Paul when they had been separated during graduate school. Paul had been out of town; it was unavoidable and therefore easier to deal with. She had continued with her life, enjoying the phone calls and letters they exchanged, sure until the final day that they would get back together.

With Alexander it was different. She still felt betrayed and angry. What was worse, she was forced to talk to him nearly every day and had to sit across the table from him during their weekly meetings making arrangements for the Upstage Theatre gala.

The preparations were proceeding better than anyone had expected. John Hamilton had agreed to direct a scene from *A Midsummer Night's Dream* and would be starring as the Devil in a portion of Shaw's *Don Juan in Hell*. The press releases were right on schedule, as were the printing of the tickets and programs. They made appeals to the long-standing core of Upstage Theatre supporters and prepared the media advertising. The ball was rolling – and it was threatening to roll right over Joanna.

In their meetings Alexander was totally distant from her, dealing out small smiles only. As November progressed, she began to think that their time together in September and October had been a period of temporary insanity, resulting in hallucinations. She could understand Alexander's reticence during the meetings, since the board and the management were generally present. It was a phone call she'd made to him that really hurt.

Sitting in her apartment on a Wednesday evening in mid-November, she forced herself to remember the call, as though pushing on a bruise to see if it still hurt.

'Hi, Alexander, it's Joanna,' she had said, feeling her blood pressure rise a few points. She hastily blamed her trembling fingers on her high intake of coffee, which had been increasing with her sleepless nights.

'Hi,' he said flatly.

'Uh, how's it going?'

'Fine.' Was all he replied.

'I just called to see whether you had a chance to look at the final versions of the press releases that are due out Friday,' she said, shaking her head and wondering how someone she thought she knew could become such a stranger to her overnight. *His voice doesn't even seem the same,* she thought with regret.

'No. Not yet.' He replied simply.

'Alexander,' she'd said hesitantly, 'I have to have your okay by tomorrow; otherwise we'll miss the deadline.'

'You'll get your okay. I'm in the middle of five hundred things and the press releases have fallen to one side. I'm sorry, but I have work to do and nobody else can do it.'

Joanna had felt anger rise in her and hadn't even tried to contain it. 'Listen, you may have five *million* things to do to get ready for the gala, but if you don't okay these press releases by tomorrow and get me some answers to that stuff we talked about in the meeting last week, you won't even have an audience.'

'You'll get everything you need tomorrow morning In the meantime; I have to get back to my five hundred things. Okay?' His voice had become hard as a rock and it seemed to Joanna that he was holding her personally responsible for the five hundred things he had to do.

'Gee, I'm terribly sorry to have wasted your time,' she'd ended up saying, even though she knew that she shouldn't let her ill temper match his own.

'So am I.' and with that he had hung up with an angry click.

Since then, their conversations had been civil at best. There was no hint of affection they had once shared and Joanna was rapidly concluding she'd been right in thinking they were through for good. It now seemed that there was absolutely no way that after the gala she and Alexander could pick up their relationship where it had left off. They both bristled when forced to speak to each other and every single word seemed to be misunderstood.

Chalk up another one to experience, Joanna, she thought wearily, pouring herself another cup of tea. *Who wouldn't be hurt if a relationship was destroyed in the name of professionalism,* she wondered, blowing on the hot brew.

And who wouldn't be hurt if one of the parties in question gave in without a fight? Under the hurt was sheer anger, anger with Upstage Theatre for having laid such ground rules, anger with Alexander for having accepted them, anger that she had no control over the situation. She was also feeling an overwhelming frustration with the whole situation and a kind of frightened confusion.

Will the real Alexander Carlson please stand up? She thought. *Which is the real one' The loving man I knew earlier or this person I hardly recognise?* It was unacceptable that one person should haves such opposite extremes.

I don't like Alexander, she thought, knowing she was trying to protect herself. *And I don't love him, either!* Had he been in the room, she might have stuck out her tongue at him.

By the last Saturday in November, Joanna was wondering whether she would survive December. If it hadn't been for her small support system, she would really have wondered. As it was, she had those people to thank for what remained of her sanity.

Bill had been helpful all along. She had been over to his house three times that month, much more often than usual. Both he and Sandy seemed to understand what she was going through and did their best to distract her. Their two children's antics often cheered her up enough to allow her to rejuvenate and put her feet back on the ground.

The night before, she had gone to her parents for support, the kind of special love that she received only from the people who had known her from babyhood. There had never been a great chasm between Joana and her parents, even during her rebellious college days. Whether they saw each other twice a week or twice a month, they always seemed to get along and they had become progressively closer as Joanna grew older.

'I've come home to Mother, Mom,' Joanna had announced as she entered the small, neat brick house in West Sydney where she had grown up.

'Things still not too pleasant between you and Alexander?' her mother had asked.

'You guessed it,' Joanna had answered, tears welling in her eyes. Tears were always quick to come to the surface when she was with her mother and something was troubling her.

Ellie Marsh put one hand up to her daughter's cheek. 'You just remember that it's his loss, dear. Do you want to move back here?' she had teased. It was a family joke her mother had used in such situations ever since Joanna had purchased her condo.

'Yeah. I would, except that Dad's still allergic to Alexander the Great.'

'Well, remember, your room's still there for you any time you want to come home.'

'Thanks, Mom. I may take you up on that.' The thought had been tempting. 'Oh, by the way, I've reserved you and Dad tickets for the opening night of the gala.'

'Will Alexander be there? I can't wait to met the man and give him a good kick in the pants for having been so nasty to my one and only daughter'

Joanna had smiled at the thought of her mother's fiery temper erupting in such a swy. 'It's not entirely his fault, Mom. Jim suggested we separate. The problem was that Alexander agreed to do so.'

'And you think that was cowardly?'

'I wish I could think that it wasn't.'

That night at dinner her father asked, 'What are your plans for Christmas?'

'I haven't made any plans. I've been so wrapped up with the theatre that I didn't realise Christmas was getting so close. I also know that we will be working right up until the last minute around Christmas, so I won't have any time off.'

'Well, your brother will be here for Christmas and will be arriving on December twenty-third. Is there any chance you could take the twenty-fourth and twenty-sixth off so you could spend some time with us over the holidays?'

'I'll see what I can arrange. Maybe Bill will look after Alexander the Great for those days. I know his kids love animals, so don't think that will be a problem.'

It's nice to be with people who are unconditionally on your side, Joanna thought when she was back in her condo the next day. She could always count on her parents to stick up for her, no matter what. And right now, she needed that.

She sighed and looked out the window at the Sydney street below. They'd had a shower overnight and the heat and high humidity had gone. The clouds had gone, allowing rays of sunlight to penetrate the gray and her spirits rose with the sunshine. *Well, well,* she mused. *I'd better take advantage of this. A long walk will do me good.*

She grabbed her umbrella and tramped down the street, her eyes roving across the small businesses in the neighbourhood. The sun slipped behind a cloud, but was out again in a few minutes. The warmth and light cast deep shadows. She enjoyed looking at window boxes on apartments full of spring flowers that had opened wide with the rain and sunshine.

Letting herself go where her feet led her, she walked on and on. An hour and a half passed with astonishing speed. She was at the Sydney centre where as a teenager she had attended the 2000 Sydney Olympics. The Convention Centre was a very busy place with several exhibition halls, an auditorium and further along she passed a soccer stadium.

She took a seat on the ledge around a huge fountain. The spigots arranged around the fountain base sprayed high plumes of water, accompanied by the strains of Beethoven's Sixth Symphony from the loudspeakers at the foot of the fountain.

This fountain had always been one of Joanna's favourite places. Sitting there with the light spray on her face brought back memories of her life in Sydney: Bill Timmerman, her first high-school sweetheart; the summer days when she played clarinet with the All-City Marching Band, the weekly practices in the concert hall; and Paul.

Breaking up with Paul was like a picnic compared to now, she thought. With Paul, one fell swoop and the whole thing was over, except for a Christmas card printed in Spanish and postmarked Madrid. She realised that she no longer held any great grudges against Paul. In fact, she felt nothing other than a dull ache for the lost years. There was no anger, no love and no real interest in what he was doing or what he had become.

Her growing-up years, college, Paul – all gone, all past. She felt very old.

Restless again, she rose and continued her walk. As soon as she passed through the iron gates of the Centre, she knew where she was going. She was going to walk past Upstage Theatre, just to look at the old brick building with its steep, red-carpeted stairs. The four blocks of parking lots and restaurants were hazy in front of her eyes as she tried to convince herself that Upstage Theatre was the last edifice in the world she wanted to see

Now it was in front and to the right of her. Lights in the back of the theatre shone in the daylight across the concave surface of the old alleyway. People were working inside, weekend though it was.

The heavy front doors opened and two people came out. One of them was Alexander. Joanna fought an impulse to hide behind a parked car. Instead, she leaned nonchalantly against a tree. They couldn't see her where she stood. Unable to resist, again feeling as though she were testing a bruise, she looked around the tree.

Alexander carried a clipboard and some file folders. He was dressed in a respectable pair of blue jeans and a tweed jacket of soft heather blue against beige and grey. The usual blue work shirt hugged his strong shoulders and chest. Joanna felt her pulse speed up.

And with Alexander was a woman, a blonde woman in a camel-coloured pantsuit and a chocolate-brown blouse that looked like silk. They descended the steps and walked down the street in the opposite direction, talking animatedly. Joanna could hear the deep tones of Alexander's voice juxtaposed with the lighter ones of the woman's. Her heart jumped in her throat as she saw Alexander throw his right arm around the woman's shoulders.

She turned away, not wanting to see him kiss the woman on the forehead, which she knew he did in such a situation. She walked quickly up the block and turned back towards her condo. *He certainly didn't wait long,* She thought cynically. *I suppose that woman is with the theatre. What about conflict of interest and professionalism there?*

Part of her was angry and jealous. The rest of her felt as though she had received a double dose of betrayal. Now her wariness took over completely. She could almost feel her internal walls going up again to protect herself.

Halfway to her condo, it began to rain, but she scarcely noticed. In a daze she let herself into her condo, fed Alexander the Great, made herself a cup of tea and retreated to her bedroom. At random, she selected one of Dean Koontz's books hoping to divert her enough from reality. In the past his books had helped her through her adjustment to college after high school, her adjustment to the 'real world' after college – and her break-up with Paul. Every large change in her life had been buffered by those eternal fictional characters and the intrigue of their stories.

Still numb but now content, Joanna read on, pausing only to turn on the light.

When she closed the book slowly and looked at the clock, it was one-thirty in the morning. She uncurled herself from the bed, stretching the muscles that had been in the same position for nearly eight hours. Alexander the Great was curled up in a ball on his blue pillow in the corner of the bedroom, snoring lightly. She picked him up. She knew if she was careful, he wouldn't even wake up. She buried her face in his warm, sleeping-cat-scented body. He uncoiled himself and lay in her arms, a limp bundle of fur.

'You sweetie,' she whispered, putting him gently back down on his pillow.

She walked into her lounge room, feeling as though she were emerging from a trance. Her condo was cheery and just as she wanted it to be. Everything was where she had put it, where it should be. It was a reflection of what she was like inside. She smiled. *I'll survive,* she told herself firmly.

She fixed herself another cup of tea, made some toast and took a seat on the sofa. Her fictional friends had helped her again. Her soul had been diverted from her melancholy and that was all that mattered.

'As of now, she said aloud, 'not only will I *look* like a professional advertising woman, I will *be* a professional advertising woman. There's no way I'm going to allow any man, regardless of who he is, to take control of my life. There's nothing Alexander can do that will ever get to me again.

She felt like Scarlett O'Hara shaking her fist in the radish field and vowing that she'd never be hungry again. No, she wouldn't ever be hungry again for a smile – or a kiss – from Alexander. It was finished.

That Something Special

Chapter Ten

On December fifth, Joanna walked into her office and started to get a cup of coffee when the phone rang.

'Joanna, it's Tom.' He sounded harried. We've got an emergency meeting with Upstage Theatre this morning. Your car or mine?'

'Mine,' Joanna answered. 'What's going on?'

'I have no idea. I'll meet you in the parking lot in five minutes.' Tom said, 'They'd better not decide to scrap the gala. But I wouldn't put it past them.'

'You really don't know what's going on?' Joanna asked as they waited for a traffic light.

'Honestly.'

Jim Melrose met them at the entrance to the theatre. On the way down the aisle to the front row of seats, Joanna heard him mumble, 'This has got to work. We're going to be sunk if it doesn't.' She looked at Tom. He raised his eyebrows and shrugged.

Five people were already seated. Joanna saw Alexander with the same blond woman, who was now introduced as Rosemary Pastor, the actress playing Jean Rice in *The Entertainer.* The other three people were also connected with the segment of the gala. A young man named Brett was to play Frank Rice and Janet Bryan would be Phoebe.

John Hamilton, direct from the National Theatre was also present. He was very tall, with strong British features that Joanna could tell would show up well under harsh stage lights. When they were introduced, he engulfed Joanna's hand in one of his huge ones and said, '*Very* pleased to meet you.' His eyes were too sincere.

Joanna and Tom sat down and accepted cups of coffee. Jim leaned against the raised platform of the stage. 'Well, we're all her now,' he said.

'No we're not,' Brett said. 'Where's Joe?'

'Sorry to keep all of you in suspense,' Jim went on, 'but I wanted everyone involved to be here before I started.' He heaved a sigh that shook his small frame. 'We've got a terrible problem, my friends. Joe Wolston – Joanna and Tom, he's the lead in *The Entertainer* got hurt over the weekend.'

'Oh no!' Rosemary gasped. 'What happened?'

'He and his wife and kids got into a four-car pileup. The car was totalled, his wife has a concussion and his two kids have bumps and bruises. Joe broke his upper arm, five ribs and dislocated his left shoulder. And his left wrist is broken.'

'Blast!' Alexander said. Joanna looked at him closely for the first time. He looked pale and strained.

Jim continued, 'He's at St. Vincent's Hospital. They had to put some pins into him and he can't be moved just yet.'

There were murmurs of sympathy from everyone. 'I'll have to take up a collection from the theatre to send him and his wife some flowers,'

Rosemary said. For some reason, she reminded Joanna of an overgrown cheerleader.

'I hate to sound cold hearted,' John Hamilton said in his low, resonant voice, 'but that puts us in a bind now doesn't it? Who's going to be Archie Rice?'

'Well, we could put the understudy in the part,' Jim suggested.

John shook his head. 'No. I've seen him in rehearsal for *A Midsummer Night's Dream.* He's good, but he's too young. He couldn't carry it off.'

'I had a feeling you'd say that, Johnny,' Jim commented. 'That's why I invited our friends from Craft-Marker here today. What I'm about to say will affect them too.'

Joanna saw Alexander straighten up in his chair. She could feel the wariness radiate from him.

'No, Jim. No way.' He said with finality.

'Alexander, you've got to.' Jim said.

'What are you talking about?' Rosemary asked. Her question was ignored.

'I'm an administrator,' Alexander said, 'and sometimes other things, but I am definitely no longer an actor.'

'You did *The Entertainer* in New York. It says so on your résumé.'

'I don't care.' Alexander seemed more upset than Joanna had ever seen him. His face had coloured deeply and the hand that held the coffee cup trembled. 'The production was a flop and it was so far off Broadway that it was practically in New Jersey. It was nearly solely responsible for the breakup of my marriage and I played Frank, not Archie. I won't do it.'

Joanna heard Rosemary gasp when Alexander mentioned his marriage. She herself felt like gasping, since she knew that Alexander, although not reticent, was not particularly outspoken with most people. After all, the only thing he'd ever said to her about his marriage was that his ex-wife had been against the idea of having children. She looked at him. He was studying the contents of his coffee cup. Something in his posture made Joanna think that he was regretting his outburst.

Even Jim seemed somewhat ill at ease. 'I'm sorry about the effect the play had on your personal life, Alex, but you still know the show. And this is only one scene. 'Actually only part of one scene. You've got to do it!

'No!'

'Yes!'

Oh, don't you guys start that routine now, Joanna thought with a sigh. It could go on for hours.

'Jim, what about my job? You know, the one that has the title of creative director? I have a lot of work to do. Who is going to do it if I'm learning Archie?'

'That's why Tom and Joanna are here,' Jim said. 'Tom, would you lend us Joanna for the afternoons until the gala goes up? She can work in one of the offices here.' Jim said. '

Tom seemed taken aback. 'Jim I really don't know what to say. That's a pretty unusual request, you know.'

'Don't worry. You'll be compensated. I've already talked to the board of directors about it. They've okayed an extra sum to pay Craft-Marker's consultant rates for Joanna's services.'

He really knows how to put people on the spot, Joanna thought.

'Would your workload accommodate it?' Tom asked Joanna.

She looked at her supervisor, silently beseeching him not to put her in the position of having to make the decision. A minute passed, an uncomfortable moment of silence laden with heavy thoughts. 'I could probably handle my accounts in the mornings, Tom, but I think it is a little premature even to be discussing this, since it doesn't appear that Alexander's going to take the part.'

'Alexander's going to take the part,' Jim said, speaking each word distinctly.

'I am not.' Alexander said.

'You are. What kind of contract do you have with Upstage Theatre, Alex?' Jim's voice was quiet and firm.

Alexander sighed and shook his head. 'You know as well as I do,' he said, his voice resigned. 'It's open-ended so that I can do other things besides being creative director.'

'Is acting excluded from the contract?'

'No, but it's not included, either.'

'It is now. Hello, Archie.'

Alexander looked steadily at Jim. Joanna could feel his anger. 'Blast you, Jim,' he whispered.

'The show must go on, Alex. You know that as well as anybody.'

'Yeah, regardless of anybody's feelings. That attitude is exactly why I quit acting.'

'I say, it's only for a month, Alex,' John Hamilton said. 'I'll bring you a copy of the script when we're through here. You won't have any trouble at all.'

'Well Joanna,' Jim said, turning his attention to her now, 'do we have the pleasure of your company for a month?'

Joanna looked at Tom. He nodded. She nodded to Jim. It was the last thing she wanted to do, to spend twenty hours a week at the theatre while Alexander had fits of artistic temperament and chased after Rosemary. But it seemed that she had no choice.

'I guess so,' she said.

'Terrific! Thanks so much. You've really bailed us out. Upstage Theatre gives you its undying gratitude.'

'Never believe a thing the man says, Joanna,' Alexander warned. 'Look what he did to me.'

'Come, come now, Alex. Show Joanna where your office is and then we can get down to business. Take five everybody.'

Alexander motioned Joanna to follow him. They went out past the ticket office, up a few stairs and into the wings of the stage. Rosemary lounged against a door prop drinking a glass of water. Joanna tried to ignore her and her accusing eyes.

'So that's why all the actresses at Upstage Theatre are frustrated, eh, Alexander?' Rosemary said. 'Because little Alex doesn't like actresses any more?'

Alexander stopped. 'Be quiet, Rosemary.'

'He prefers professional women, eh? Well, I sure do feel privileged that he even deigned to take me out on Saturday.'

'If I'd known what a snake you are, you would have paid for your own coffee,' he said.

Joanna was embarrassed for him. 'Come on, Alexander,' she murmured, pushing lightly at his elbow.

'How touching! She stands up for him!' Rosemary said with false emotion.

'Oh shut up, Rosemary,' Alexander said. He took Joanna's arm and pulled her along after him down the corridor. He opened the door and stood aside to let Joanna enter. He avoided her eyes.

'This is my office,' he said, waving at a paper-strewn desk. One small window in back of the desk looked onto the alley. Other than the desk chair, there was one other, covered with file folders. A dusty file cabinet stood along the wall. 'Most of the stuff concerning the gala is on the desk and you might as well dredge through it yourself, since there's little order to the chaos. Anything that's not on the desk is on the chair, but a lot of that has to do with the summer season.'

'Thanks, Alexander. I'm sorry this has happened.'

His eyes finally met hers. 'Thank you too, Jo. I'm sorry if I've seemed like a creep.'

She shrugged. 'Under the circumstances, that may have been the best way to go about it. Anyway, don't worry. I'm just sorry that you're stuck with acting again.'

For a few moments he was silent, as if considering something. Finally he said, 'I've got to tell you about my marriage, if you can handle it. I could feel your mind asking a million questions in there and I have to thank you for not have gasped the way Rosemary did.'

'You don't have to, Alexander. It's up to you.'

'If you remember, one of my bad habits was telling you everything that came into my head. I'm all right when you're not around, but the minute you are, the old gut-spilling instinct takes over again.'

He took a deep breath. 'In a nutshell, my wife left me for another man. We were in the production of *The Entertainer*. Ginny fell in love with Peter, the guy who played Archie. They had a torrid affair from the second day of rehearsals. It was completely humiliating. The whole time, rehearsals and performances, was a disaster. I decided to give Ginny another chance when we left the show, because I don't give up easily. But she wasn't interested. She wanted to marry Peter and have a family. She'd always refused to have *my* kids.'

How horrible! Joanna thought. How could anyone *not* want to have Alexander's kids? How could anyone be that cruel? 'I can see why *The*

Entertainer would be the last show you would want to be in,' she said.

'No kidding! Anyway, I just wanted you to know the true story, in case Rosemary decides to start rumours. I wouldn't put it past her.'

'Yes. I've heard that rumours travel like wildfire in the theatre.

'That's true.'

Alexander looked at Joanna. The silence became awkward. His eyes were as green as ever, his body was built the same and he even smelled as before. Joanna unconsciously shook her head.

'Why did you shake your head?' he asked.

'I didn't know I had.'

'You did. Everything will be all right. We can handle working together, Jo. Don't worry about it.'

He had indeed read her mind. 'I don't know, Alex. It's not going to be easy.'

'Who said that life would be easy? We'll do all right.'

John and Rosemary were at the door.

'Five minutes are up, Alex,' John said as he entered the office, his bulk seeming to fill the cramped space. 'Here.' He handed Alexander a paperbound book with an orange cover.

'Thanks a lot,' Alexander said sarcastically.

Joanna turned to go. 'See you tomorrow,' she said.

John looked at her. 'I'm looking forward to working with you Miss Marsh,' he said, too warmly.

'Sorry if we interrupted anything.' Rosemary said waspishly.

'No problem,' Joanna said. 'Good-bye.'

As they drove back to Craft-Marker, Joanna was quiet. Tom had said, 'Sorry,' in a kindly way as they started off, but otherwise he, too, remained silent.

After a few blocks, she sighed and said, 'It's going to be miserable, Tom.'

'I got that impression. But you'll do fine, I'm sure of it.'

'I wish I were sure.'

Chapter Eleven

By the end of her second week of half days spent on the Upstage Theatre premises, Joanna could understand why Alexander had been short with her over the phone. Even though she did her best to concentrate on the many things she had to do, the theatre environment interrupted her time and time again. She longed for her calm, quiet office and for more than one reason she dreaded the afternoon hours when she would have to be near Alexander in the madhouse that Upstage Theatre was becoming.

From time to time she had visitors in her office. Alexander would stop by during breaks to stare at his script, mouthing the words of the scene over and over again. Since she had appropriated his office, she assumed he was there only because he had nowhere else to study. Nevertheless, his presence was disturbing. Rosemary stopped by too, ostensibly looking for Alexander. But she left after making probing, catty remarks about him and Joanna that were obviously motivated by jealousy and frustration.

John Hamilton was increasingly in evidence. He was ostensibly looking for Rosemary, but his invitations to Joanna to join him for a drink or dinner left her with no doubt about his intentions towards her. The situation resembled something out of the theatre of the absurd and Joanna wondered if

Rosemary and John thought they were pulling the wool over her eyes.

The constant flurry of activity that passed through the office section of the theatre was more insidiously distracting than the unwelcome visitors. Actors and actresses were, she found, just about the noisiest group of people imaginable. They were obviously all performers. They all loved being in the spotlight and had a seemingly insatiable need for attention. This was reflected in their raucous behaviour as they went down the halls, breaking into song or dance or telling theatre anecdotes. The theatre was a self-contained gossip mill and some amorous adventure seemed always to be the topic of conversation.

Joanna, in her more hopeful moments, thought that she should find the environment stimulating, but in fact it left her bone-weary and drained at the end of each day. Bit by bit, the casual contact she had with Alexander at the theatre came to be enough for her and she was almost relieved that she did not have to worry about a relationship which would have robbed her of the little energy she had left. It was just as well there was 'all work and no play' between them, because they were under so much stress that they would probably have had problems.

It's all for the best, she thought, *We would have been so pooped by this time that we wouldn't have seen much of each other anyway.*

On Friday night at five, she gathered up her papers, organising them in her briefcase. She left the office door unlocked, since Alexander had not yet finished for the evening and would need to get his things. In the hall, she pushed against the huge cast of *A Midsummer Night's Dream,* who were flocking to the bulletin board to look at the director's notes for the next day.

'Dinnertime. What shall we put in our tummies tonight, children?' said one of the male sprites bouncily. A chorus of different culinary choices deafened Joanna.

Behind the *Midsummer Night's Dream* cast followed, at a slower pace, the five-person cast and the director of *The Entertainer.* There was no way Joanna could avoid the contact with all three of the people she least wanted to see; Rosemary, John and Alexander. Soon she was engulfed in a theatrical bear hug from the effusive John. 'Oh love, you've got to come out for a drink with us tonight,' he said. 'We have so much to celebrate.'

'What's that?' Joanna asked tiredly.

'Oh, Joanna, you must know how brilliant, how positively stunning Alexander is as Archie,' John gushed. 'Or haven't you sat in on any of the rehearsals? No, I guess not. Well, take it from me, he is absolutely marvellous.' The other members of the cast nodded appreciatively, while Alexander stood quietly. Joanna couldn't tell what sort of look was on his face; it was expressionless and that made her nervous.

'Anyhow, I told him today that I'm *sure* we could find a place for him at the National and that he must, just *must* come back to London with me after the gala for an audition.'

Joanna thought that after everything that had happened in the past two months she had become impervious to pain, to quick, unchecked reactions. She was wrong. In an instant, she imagined the press release headline: *Alexander Carlson, formerly of Sydney's Upstage Theatre, accepts position with England's National Theatre.* No doubt she would have to do the publicity for it.

She looked directly at Alexander. 'Are you going to do it?' She was terrified of hearing his answer, although she was so angry that she almost didn't care what he said.

'I don't know, Jo,' he said quietly. 'It's quite an opportunity.'

Nearly in tears, she brushed past them. 'Best of luck, Alex. Send me a postcard if you think of it.'

As soon as she was out of sight, she broke into a run, ignoring Alexander's call of, 'Joanna, wait!'

She did not stop until she reached the parking lot and her car. She leaned against the door, breathless with exertion, anger and the effort it took to keep tears at bay. A figure bounded across the parking lot and soon Alexander was beside her. She looked around, feeling like a trapped animal, but there was nowhere she could run.

'Joanna, John just made the offer tonight. I didn't accept anything,' he said, trying to catch his breath.

'What's the difference? You know how actors are,' she said. 'You're crazy about the spotlight and once you've been bitten by the bug you never recover. I'm amazed you were able to resist as long as you have. I would never expect you to pass up the chance to make the same mistakes you made ten years ago.' She looked at him defiantly, knowing she had hurt him. She didn't care; in fact, she was glad. 'I mean, you're no different from all the rest.'

'You think so, eh? he said coldly. 'I thought you knew me better than that, but if that's the way you want to look at it, okay. I'll send you a postcard, if I remember.'

He continued in a softer voice, 'No doubt your future boyfriend will be a good, steady insurance broker or real-estate agent with all the imagination and creativity of a single chair leg. You can tell him you got burned by two guys who went off and left you in the lurch. That's what hurts, isn't it, Joanna?' His voice had become tenderer and he reached up to push an unruly curl away from her face.

Joanna, however, was not that easily placated. 'It's none of your business what I do, Alexander. Have fun in London, as I said and in the meantime I wish you and Rosemary all the best.'

'Joanna, you're crazy.'

'No, Alexander, you are. Good-bye. I'll try to see to it that we have as little contact as possible until this whole misbegotten gala is out of the way.'

He looked at her wryly, almost amused. 'This whole 'misbegotten gala' was your idea.'

'Actually, it was *our* idea, so you're partially responsible too.'

'Jo, we're being so silly. Forget it. I won't go to London. I don't want to act anyway.' His voice was soft, the voice of Alexander she had loved.

Joanna had the feeling that if he said one more kind word to her she'd burst into tears. 'As I said, Alexander,' she concluded wearily, 'what's the difference? It's over between us anyway, thanks to Jim and the board of directors. And thanks to your kindly obliging them. Do what you want to do.'

'Is it over, Joanna?' he asked. 'Do you really think so?'

'Didn't you make sure it was?' she retorted.

Alexander jerked her car door open in a new display of anger. 'Fine. I'll send you a postcard from London.

Joanna climbed into her car and Alexander slammed the door shut. She started the engine with a roar and, tires spinning, gravel flying, she pulled out of the parking lot, the tears now flowing down her cheeks.

Joanna spent the whole weekend thinking. She contemplated herself into a state of fatigue and emotional exhaustion and not even a thick coating of foundation makeup could conceal on Monday morning that she had an awful weekend.

On impulse, she called Tom Dobson's personal assistant to see if Tom was available. He was and immediately invited her up to his office.

'Hi, Joanna,' he said as she entered. 'What can I do for you? Everything going all right with the gala?'

She sank into a chair. 'Yes and no, Tom. Working there at the theatre is crazy. The actors are so distracting and their excess energy sort of bounces off the walls. It's impossible to stay calm and cool with fifteen sprites from *A Midsummer Night's Dream* flitting around.

Tom shook his head and laughed at her description. 'Sounds like your typical theatre. Funny, that's one thing that really doesn't change much. In college, the theatre people were exhibitionists who delighted in being noncon-formists. By the time they reach the level of professional theatre, their eccentricities are at least as well developed as their art. At least, that's true of the bit players. The really great ones never need to be eccentric.'

'Yeah, I guess,' she said absently.

'Joanna, you look absolutely bushed. Why don't you take a few days off after the gala's over?'

'Actually, I was going to ask you whether I could take a couple of extra days off during Christmas. My brother is coming home for Christmas and I would like to be there over the holidays. I would need a couple of extra days from Tuesday, December twenty-third until Saturday December twenty-seventh.'

'That's only two days more than usual. Of course you can – you will be able to revitalise yourself and be raring to go again for when the gala starts. But I also think you should seriously think about taking some time off after the gala to have a proper holiday.'

139

She looked up at him, surprised. 'That's exactly what I wanted to talk to you about. In addition to the days over Christmas, I could really use a proper vacation.'

'Sure, no problem. Let's see.' He looked at his desk calendar.' The dates for the gala are January the ninth through eleventh and sixteenth through eighteenth. Then the theatre starts its normal summer season. Is that taken care of?'

Joanna nodded. 'The campaign for the gala pretty much encompasses the summer season as well, since the goal is slowly to change the theatre's repertoire and image. One takes care of the other.'

'The last night of the gala, then, is January eighteenth, a Sunday night. When do you want to go on vacation?'

'How about Monday, January nineteenth?' She asked, smiling glumly.

'Fine. For how long?'

'How long can I have?' Joanna was beginning to enjoy this game of negotiating, especially since it seemed she could have anything she wanted.

'Name it.' Tom said grinning.

'Two years.' She replied as she too grinned at the silliness of her idea.

'How about two weeks?'

'You've got a deal. I'll be back to work on Monday February second.'

'What are you going to do?'

Joanna smiled as though the world was her oyster and she could not decide out of the endless possibilities. 'I don't know. I may go to Cairns and SCUBA dive off the Quicksilver boat; or maybe go to Paris and find a rich, French nobleman ... or I may go to Mexico and have a siesta every afternoon ... or I may just stay here and do my spring cleaning, which I still haven't done I've been so busy.'

'Oh, not that!' Tom teased.

'You're probably right. Although at this point the mere thought that I will no longer in any way have to deal with the sprites and decrepit music-hall performers and French parasites of the eighteenth century and Shaw's Devil, gives me such joy that I can hardly stand it.'

'That must just be wild,' Tom said, shaking his head again. 'One day you'll have to write a book about your various experiences with Craft-Marker, from Scoop 'n Eat Ice Cream to Karr's Furniture to Upstage Theatre. It'd make a best-seller.'

'Well then, maybe I'll do that while I'm relaxing on the beach in Maui for a couple of weeks.' She got to her feet. 'Thanks, Tom. I really appreciate this.'

'Any time, hon. You're doing such a terrific job on the account that you deserve a promotion and a raise on top of the vacation. Which, by the way, even though I shouldn't be telling you, you can count on looking forward to, too.'

'Wow! Maybe suffering does have its rewards. All the same, I won't hold you to the promotion and the raise. The vacation is the only essential.'

'Hey, come on. Virtue must be rewarded too, not just suffering. Anyway, you don't want to stay where you are now in the firm forever, do you?'

'I don't really mind. I'm in advertising because I like coming up with new ideas. I don't think I'd like anything that was much more administrative.'

'You really like your job that much?' Tom looked impressed. Joanna didn't lack ambition; she was content. That in itself was rare.

'Yes, I do except ...'

'...when you're being accosted by twenty-five actors in outlandish costumes,' he finished for her.

Joanna laughed. 'Exactly.'

Chapter Twelve

Joanna went into Bill Jacob's office. 'Hi Bill.'

'Hi Joanna. How are things going?'

'Hectic as usual at the Upstage Theatre. What I'm here for is to ask for your help with two things. I will be spending the Christmas holidays with my parents, but unfortunately my father is allergic to my cat. I'm wondering if you could look after him from December twenty-third till the evening of December twenty-sixth?'

'Sure, no problem. My kids love animals and that will be an extra thing they can enjoy over Christmas.'

'I was quite sure you would agree. It's the next period of time that might be far more inconvenient for you. Tom has agreed to give me two week's holidays as soon as the gala is over and I've decided to start my holidays the day after it ends. Before I make any travel plans, I wanted to make sure I had a place where little Alexander the Great could be cared for while I'm away. I'd be willing to pay while he stays with someone.'

'Joanna, we'd love to have him – no charge. We would just need you to supply whatever food he normally eats and bring his bed etc. Don't worry your little head about that problem – it's already taken care of. Now ... where do you think you will go?'

'I've been toying with several options. I'm a qualified SCUBA diver and might go to Cairns and go out on the Quicksilver boat to dive off the Great Barrier Reef. Another choice is to go to Mexico or Maui and just sit on the beach in the sun; or even something more exotic, I thought about Paris.'

'Sounds as if you have some decisions to make. I wish I was in your shoes. I could use a holiday myself, but maybe the Christmas season will rejuvenate me.'

Joanna went into work as usual at Upstage Theatre on December twenty-second and asked to speak to Jim Melrose.

'Hi Jim. I'll be away for a few days celebrating Christmas with my family starting tomorrow and including Boxing Day. I won't be back till the Monday after Christmas. My brother will be coming home and I want to spend some time with him and my parents over the holidays.'

'We'll miss you, but I can understand you wanting a few extra days away from this zoo.' He replied.

That afternoon, Joanna scoured the web and was able to find a suitable flight to Paris that went via Heathrow Airport. She booked her flight and made a copy of the E-Ticket. She also realised that it would be winter there, so on the way home she stopped to buy three warmer outfits that would be suitable for Paris weather.

The next morning Joanna delivered Alexander the Great along with his food and bed to Bill's home. They were greeted by his exuberant children who rushed to pat Alexander. 'Thanks for looking after him for me.' She said as she smiled at Bill and the children. 'Here is the phone number where I'll be staying. I'll pick him up the evening of December twenty-sixth.'

'We're so happy to have him here for the holidays,' chirped his youngest.

Joanna left knowing that he would be well cared for while she celebrated Christmas. She then drove to her parents home and lugged in all her Christmas gifts and some goodies for their holiday celebrations.

She had agreed to pick up Evan, her brother, at the Sydney Kingsford Smith Domestic Airport. He had flown in from Adelaide where he lived with his partner Jenny. Jenny had been invited too, but she had made plans to spend the time with her family in Adelaide.

Soon Jenny spotted her brother's loping strides through the airport. He was younger than her by two years and she had always felt the need to look after him. She gave him a big hug, asked about the flight then said, 'It's great seeing you again. I'm glad we will have a few days to visit over the holidays.'

'Mom said that you have been going flat-out with one of your clients – some theatre company. How is that going?'

'Don't ask. I am so tired of that group that I just want to veg out for the next few days and forget the chaos that goes on there.' she replied with a grimace.

'I would think that working with actors would be right up your alley.' He replied.

'I guess it might have been if I hadn't had such a time getting the board of directors and management people to realise that the theatre was in dire straits financially and unless they changed their repertoire, they were going to go under. It took me over two months to convince them that they should focus on other playwrights and do fewer Shakespearian and Shaw plays. They finally capitulated and agreed to do a gala. Then I got roped into doing so much for them that I had to spend the majority of my time at the theatre.'

He nodded as he collected his luggage.

'Theatre people are nuts and so noisy; I found it almost impossible to find a quiet moment to do the publicity and advertising for them. They were continually interrupting me or making so much noise out in the hallway that I lost my concentration. I finally had to ask for these extra days off to keep my sanity.' She concluded as she opened the boot of her car so he could store his luggage.

On the way to her parent's home, they chatted about this and that. As they arrived at their parent's three bedroom home, the door opened and her parents rushed to the car to welcome Evan.

'It's so good to have you here,' said her mother. 'I'm just sorry that Jenny couldn't come with you. Oh well, the four of us will have a wonderful Christmas together.'

They entered her parents lounge room to find a beautifully decorated Christmas tree with many gifts under the tree. Jenny and Evan went back to the car and brought in all their gifts to add to the pile already there.

'I smell pancakes,' said Evan. He was a great fan of his mother's buttermilk pancakes and found his mouth watering just smelling them cooking.

They all sat down and enjoyed the pancakes, bacon and coffee.

'What's new in your life Evan?' his father asked.

'I was waiting to see you to tell you, that I got another promotion.'

They all knew that Evan had been climbing the corporate ladder in the Human Resources Department in his company. 'What will you be doing at your new position?' asked Joanna.

'Well, I've filled positions in recruitment, have learned how to write job descriptions and do performance appraisal interviews and now they want me to try training. So I'll be picking your brain Joanna to give me some presentation tips you might have gleaned from watching the actors. One thing I've been practicing is projecting my voice, but still lack the self-confidence to do a real training session.'

'From what I've seen, the best actors really know their part so well they could do it in their sleep. They also spend a lot of time getting into character. I don't think that can be much different from doing training seminars. You need to know your topic inside out and want to help others by giving them that information.'

'I am researching right now to do a session for our new supervisors and managers. Most of them have been thrown into their positions without the proper training. I'm trying to think of what they need to know to do their jobs properly. My research has come up with quite a few things to explain to them.'

'One thing actors do is pick the brains of the senior actors – they seem very pleased to help the underlings do their parts well. It can't be that much different with training. Maybe you should talk to some of the managers and ask them for their input as to what they feel a supervisor needs to know to do his or her job properly.' She added.

'Thanks Joanna. Those are really good ideas and I'll do that when I get back to work.' He said as he patted her on the back. Then he turned to his parents, 'What will you two be up to in the near future?'

'We're planning another trip. This time we hope to go along the eastern seaboard from Sydney up to Cairns, then go inland a bit and come back using some of the back roads so we can really see Queensland and New South Wales. We will be going with our neighbours in their beautiful fifth-wheeler that sleeps eight people. It's just like a home on wheels and once it's parked, the sides move out and it is huge. It will be very comfortable as we travel and when we park it for the night. We will share all the expensed.' Her mother explained.

'It's going to be a great trip. We're planning on taking our laptop with us, so we can keep in touch with both of you and send you pictures as we go along.' added her father.

'How wonderful!' both Evan and Joanna replied.

Their Christmas holiday went well and they thoroughly enjoyed stuffing themselves with Christmas turkey. The normal Australian Christmas meal of cold prawns did not appeal to them – they liked having the full turkey, cranberry sauce and all the trimmings even though with the heat it was not conducive to cook a turkey inside. Her father had a big Weber barbeque that held the turkey and saved them from heating up their home.

On Boxing Day afternoon, Joanna drove Evan to the airport and returned to her parent's home for dinner.

'That was a wonderful break.' said Joanna. 'I feel wonderful and rested. I slept like a baby each night.'

'You do look much better,' her father said as he put his hand on her arm. 'I just don't like the idea that you'll be going back to that zoo and will likely have to face the same turmoil you left.'

'Well it won't be too bad, because I'll be going on holiday the day after the gala presentations are over. I leave for Paris on January nineteenth for two weeks.'

'That's great. That's about the time we will be going on our trip up north, so make sure you take your tablet with you so we can keep in touch.'

'Thanks for the wonderful time,' she said as she hugged her parents. 'Oh, I almost forgot – here are the tickets for the opening night of the play for Friday, January ninth. Do you want me to pick you up and drive you there or would you rather meet me there?'

'We can meet you there.'

Joanna waved as she drove out of their driveway. She had to pick up Alexander the Great before she went home. When she arrived at Bill's home and entered his lounge room, the children came up to her and hugged her legs. 'We've had such a good time with Alexander the Great and so glad he will be back to send *two* weeks with us soon.'

She hugged them as she said, 'Thank you very much for taking such good care of him.' Alexander the Great curled around her legs meowing to be picked up.

'And how is my little man?' She asked as she stroked him. His meow back was all the answer she needed.

When they got home, Joanna unloaded the car of cat paraphernalia and Christmas gifts then gave Alexander the Great the treat that her parents had sent for him.

Chapter Thirteen

Joanna returned to work on Friday December twenty-seventh. She had just unlocked the door when Alexander arrived.

'Where have you been?' he asked rather angrily. 'I haven't been able to get into the office since Tuesday!'

'I told Jim I would be away for a few days, so he knew where I was. Is there no extra key for the door?' she responded rather angrily herself.

'I wasn't able to find one. Now where did I put that extra script I was working on?' He said distractedly as he peered around the office. He found the pages he was looking for and stormed out of the office.

Joanna didn't see him for the rest of the day. When she returned on Monday, December thirty-first – New Year's Eve day, she wondered if he had calmed down over the weekend. The entire crew were rehearsing throughout the day, but had planned a New Year's Eve party for that evening. So the orchestra members could enjoy the party, they hired a DJ and left half the stage free where couples could dance.

Shortly after the party began, Joanna left the office, remembering not to lock it and joined the group. She had just arrived and was enjoying a glass of white wine when John took her glass, put it on a nearby table and escorted her to the dance floor.

He was a good dancer with good rhythm and they enjoyed several dances together. He was in a jovial mood and regaled her with funny stories about theatre life.

As Joanna left the dance floor she saw that Alexander was watching her. John escorted her back to her table and asked another actress to dance with him. Joanna went over to the table groaning under the myriad of food that had been set out for the party. She filled her plate and found a table next to one of the orchestra members. He introduced himself, 'Hi, I'm Danny. And you're Joanna the person in charge of publicity aren't you?'

'Yes I am. How are you enjoying the party?' she asked.

'I'm very lonely for my family. I wasn't able to get away to spend Christmas with them, so I'm feeling rather melancholy tonight, not being able to ring in the New Year with my wife and children.'

They discussed family life for a while as they finished their meals.

'Can I get you another glass of wine?' Danny asked.

'That would be very nice.' answered Joanna with a smile.

After he rose to get the wine, Joanna looked up to see Alexander approaching her, a dinner plate of food in his hand.

'Can I sit down for a minute?' he asked.

'Sure.' She replied simply.

'Did you enjoy the Christmas holidays?'

'As a matter of fact I did.' And she explained how nice it had been to spend it with her brother and parents.

'I had to leave Alexander the Great with my colleague Bill because my father is allergic to cats. They will be looking after him again when I go on holidays after the gala is over.'

'Where will you be going?' he asked.

'I'm leaning towards going to Paris. I've never been there, but if I don't get my act together there won't be any airline tickets available that I can afford.'

Danny returned with her glass of wine. Alexander stood up and said, 'I hope you have a nice trip.' And walked away.

'What was that all about?' asked Danny.

'I was just telling him about my upcoming trip to Paris.'

'That's one place I've been to. My wife and I spent our honeymoon there and it was magical. I'm sure you will love it. Will you be travelling with someone?' he asked as he sipped his vodka and tonic.

'Unfortunately, no. I would like to, but – no – I will be travelling alone.' She said sadly.

'How unfortunate. You're a lovely person and I'm surprised that you don't have someone special in your life.'

'I did have, but that's over now.' Joanna said as she felt her emotions rising.

Just then, John arrived and insisted that they have another dance. Joanna extended her hand and they enjoyed another dance set.

After their dinner, Joanna went to the ladies room and realised that she wanted to go home. She didn't want to be there at midnight when everyone else would be welcoming in the New Year. *What's to welcome?* She thought, *I'll be alone this year too, just like most of last year.*

She returned to her condo, cuddled her cat and was sound asleep by ten thirty and missed welcoming in the New Year.

Chapter Fourteen

It was Friday, January second when she returned to the theatre. Upstage Theatre was in full, frenetic swing. Opening night of the gala was just seven days away. Last-minute hammer strokes could be heard as the set people frantically repaired a door that a temperamental actor had put his foot through in a moment of anguish during a rehearsal of *The Misanthrope.*

Sewing machines hummed and actresses went from office to office in search of Band-Aids after having pricked fingers while sewing up rips and tears in costumes.

Joanna felt that she was on the edge of madness. The programs had to be reprinted because of the cast change in *The Entertainer* and the proofs were still not ready. Worse yet, the venerable members of the board of directors were becoming more and more nervous about the whole gala and would appear at her door to discuss the progress of the advertising and publicity campaigns. More than once she was tempted to say, 'Yes Mr. Talman, everything would be fine if you would just stay out of my hair and let me get my work done.' This would be unacceptable, she realised, so all she could do was keep her responses monosyllabic and hope that he and his colleagues would take the hint.

Fortunately, Alexander was nowhere to be seen, so wrapped up was he in preparing for the demanding role of Archie Rice. Rumours flowing through the theatre about his offer from the National Theatre, reached Joanna's ears despite the fact that she did her best not to hear them. The consensus was that Alexander would be a fool to pass up such an opportunity.

Rosemary was the only one to contradict the majority view, from what Joanna heard. Whether she knew something that nobody else knew or whether she was just speaking out of wishful thinking, Joanna did not know. But she did hear Rosemary say, 'Alexander won't go back to acting. Mark my words.'

As John Hamilton's nervous energy increased, so did his pursuit of Joanna. Not a day went by that he did not come into her office to petition her company after hours. He called her, 'My little other-worldly maiden with a laugh more enchanting than that of any siren or nymph.'

Joanna could only shake her head. All efforts to ward him off, seemed to go unnoticed.

The phone rang. 'Joanna, this is Jim. We've got a problem.'

'Good grief, what now?' Joanna asked. She was sick of problems.

'The story in the *Sydney Herald* gives my name as Munroe instead of Melrose. Did you do that on purpose or did someone on the paper screw up?'

'You'd better know the answer to that one, Jim,' she said shortly. Jim, she had found over the weeks, had a minor persecution complex and lapsed into self-pity at the slightest opportunity.

'I assume you mean that the paper messed up.'

'You've got it.'

'Well, what are you going to do about it?'

'I'm going to call the paper and let them know about the mistake in case they don't already know, and ask them to print a correction. Okay?'

'I'm production director of this whole gala, Joanna and they can't do this to me.'

'Jim, nobody's doing anything to you. It was an error, that's all, so just mellow out.'

Thank goodness she was so well acquainted with these people by now that she knew what she could and could not say to them. Their style was so different from that of any other professional group she'd worked with, that initially it had been like living in a foreign country, getting to know the unfamiliar customs and mores.

'I knew I could count on you to take care of it,' Jim said. 'By the way, if you see John, tell him that the cue-to-cue rehearsal for *Don Juan in Hell* is at three-thirty today.'

'That's on the notes, isn't it?'

'Yeah, but John's so busy writing his own that I doubt he even bothers to look at the ones for *Don Juan.* So tell him if you get a chance, will you?'

'Okay, I will if I see him.'

'Thanks, Joanna. You're a lifesaver,' Jim said.

Great. I'm a lifesaver, she thought as she hung up the phone. *Who's going to save my life?* She called the appropriate person at the newspaper to take care of the error and after that called the printer again to request the proofs for the program, forgetting that the printer's office would be closed by now. She slammed the phone down out of sheer frustration and then immediately checked to see whether she had done any damage. She grabbed her purse and left the office.

She walked the short distance from the theatre to the Sydney Centre and stood near the fountain. The crowd there was much larger than it had been a month earlier, thanks to the good weather. She felt that she just had to think – or rather that she had to try to empty her mind of all the details of the gala. She also had to get her mind off the possibility of Alexander's going to London permanently.

Unfortunately, she could not help herself from thinking about that. *I don't want him to go. Let him stay. Let him be smart and realise that he loves Australia, that he doesn't want to act again, and that he loves me.*

But did he love her? She doubted it – nor was she sure that she loved him any more. *Joanna, quit trying to kid yourself,* her inner voice demanded. *You know quite well that you love him more than you've ever loved anybody and although you want him to be happy in his career; you don't want him to be happy thousands and thousands of kilometres away from you.*

What was this urge that made people want to live so far away from where they were born? Or travel so far away for long periods of time? She could not have done it, of that she was certain. She loved Australia, her family, her home, her life-style and her cat. She couldn't leave. She had ties here.

Did no one else? Did it bother others that they had no roost - no home?

Home: where did she feel most at home? The house where Alexander lived. That place had been home to her the first time she saw it. How could it not be to Alexander, who had lived there most of his life? At least Paul had been out of Sydney for a while, had chosen to get into a field that demanded he go abroad. Alexander had no such excuse.

She returned to the theatre resigned to her confusion. It would not end she knew, until Alexander actually made his decision and was on the plane bound for London. But a small part of her still hoped, wished and even prayed that he would not go.

Instead of going back to the cluttered office with its dreary view of the dingy alleyway, she walked up the steps into the auditorium itself. A rehearsal of *The Entertainer* was in progress. *I've got to see for myself how good he is,* she thought as she took a seat in the darkened back row.

Alexander sat in an armchair, Rosemary beside him. As he began to speak, Joanna noticed that he was not using his script.

'Stop Alex,' John Hamilton said, rising from his seat in the front row. His voice carried clearly to Joanna. 'You can't *do* it that way. I've told you before that it doesn't work.'

Joanna was now seeing a different side of John. His language was direct and his accent was crisp and precise, unlike the slightly slurred, decadent one he used when he called Joanna his nymph. She watched, fascinated with this careful creation of what the audience would see.

'This is just about the only time in the show that Archie isn't performing,' John continued. 'He *can't* use the same voice and mannerisms he's used for the rest of the scene. Now let's try it again, shall we?'

At the same point in the scene, John stopped Alexander again, 'Are you just being stubborn or are you incapable of doing what I ask?'

'John, if Archie changes too much, the scene won't be believable,' Alexander said, standing up.

'Well, then, we just have different points of view on the subject, Alex my boy. And since I'm the director, you're there to take my direction. Won't you do it my way? It'll make it much easier for all concerned, I assure you.'

'You know I've directed before, John and you *are wrong.* I'm taking a break.'

Joanna shrank down in her seat, hoping that he wouldn't see her as he charged up the aisle to her right. After a few minutes, during which John and Rosemary rehearsed the scene, Joanna rose and took a circuitous route back to the office.

She didn't know the play, so she couldn't judge which approach to the scene was better. But she had seen the remarkable performance of *TheTempest* that Alexander had directed. On the strength of that, she had faith that he was correct and that in the end he would do the scene his way, with or without John's approval.

By Friday, the programs had still not been approved or printed. The atmosphere at the theatre was completely mad. The energy touched everyone who came in contact with it, Joanna included. She was ready to go down to the printer personally and turn the crank on the press if that was what it took. She had been calm, trying to impress upon the printer the importance of time in this matter in a businesslike way. When that had not worked, she had proceeded from pleading to yelling, to threatening to remove the job from the firm and back to pleading again.

Meanwhile, she had a million other things to do and she was completely engrossed in them when the phone rang. It was the printer, saying that the proofs were ready to be checked. She was waiting for four important media people to return her calls, so she knew she could not go to the printer's immediately. It was already three-thirty in the afternoon. She hung up with a promise to be there as soon as possible.

What was she going to do? The change was minor, just putting Alexander's name in place of Joe's on the page featuring *The Entertainer.* That was why she had become so irate about the delay in the first place. Still, she didn't trust anyone else to do the job except Alexander and asking him was out of the question.

John entered her office and she had to bite back the urge to tell him to go away and leave her alone.

'How's my little wood sprite today, eh?' he asked kissing her. She wanted to wipe it off.

'Wonderful. And how's the Devil?' she asked referring to his role in *Don Juan in Hell.*

'The heck if I know,' he said, chuckling appreciatively at his own joke.' But you look as though you're ready to go through the ceiling. What's the matter? Haven't those nasty old printers finished with the programs yet?'

'They just called to tell me that the proofs are ready to be checked, but I don't know when I'll be able to get there, because I'm waiting for calls from Dan Linzberg and Guy Peterson and K-ART radio and ...'

'Can I do it? Honestly, love, I'd be happy to.'

Joanna looked at him incredulously. He was actually offering to help when he was involved in two portions of the gala?

'No John, you must have a thousand things to do yourself.'

'Really, it's no problem. The only change is the name change, isn't it?'

'Yes, but I still wanted to look over the whole thing to make sure they don't miss anything the first time around.'

'Give me the address of the printer and tell me how to get there. I'll check the proofs, okay them if they're all right and bring you back a copy before five o'clock. How does that sound?' He looked at her winningly, his huge dark brown eyes so persuasive that Joanna felt slightly relieved.

'John, if you could, I'd be so grateful. You're about the only person I'd trust with this, since you're directly involved with *The Entertainer.* Alexander would be ideal, but I don't think he's available. 'Are you sure you can do it?'

'You're right, Alexander isn't available. He's still dropping lines from the end of the scene, so I've sent him to a corner of the dressing room to finish his work. And I've already told you three times that I'd be most happy to help.'

Here he paused, making Joanna suspicious. 'On condition that you go with me to the opening-night party.'

'I wasn't invited,' she protested, knowing it was a weak excuse. 'I didn't even plan it. Jim decided he wanted to be social chairman, so I let him take care of the details.'

'You've been invited now. I know you'd rather go with Alexander, but he's a bit tied up with little Rosemary right at the moment. I think I can bear being second choice; at least I can hope that someday I'll be first in your heart.' He stuck a tragic pose and then relaxed as though realising how idiotic he looked. 'Do we have a deal?'

'We have a deal,' she said, reaching across the desk to shake the large hand. She gave him the printer's address. He made his exit triumphantly with a wave of his hand saying, 'Ta-ta, love. See you in a bit.'

Joanna sat back in her chair and fumed. *Well, of all the rotten things for Alexander to do! I was right about him and Rosemary. Well, fine. I'll just see them at the party.*

At four-thirty John returned; the proof sheets in hand. 'They're perfect, Joanna. You had nothing to worry about. Look for yourself.' He gave her the proofs.

Joanna looked at the typeface carefully, at the spelling of each character's name and corresponding actor's name; she checked the format against her notes on the subject, and then glanced at John with a grin. 'Fantastic. They *are* perfect. Now, when will they all be ready?'

'By the end of the day tomorrow. They're the number-one priority for the shop right now. So you have nothing to worry about.'

'Thank goodness. And thank you, John, for having gone there for me. I've gotten three out of the four phone calls I was waiting for and I never would have if I'd had to go do that.'

'The pleasure was all mine, my sweet.' He leaned across the desk and put his hand on her cheek, his eyes more serious than she had ever seen them. 'You really are sweet, you know. So hard working, so dedicated. I'd love for you to be dedicated to me.'

'Aw, come off it, you charmer,' Joanna said, feeling ill-at-ease with this new mood of John's.

'Oh well, some things are meant to be and other things are not. Still, I'm glad the programs are all right and I'm glad I could help. Besides,' he added with a grin, 'the reward far surpasses the effort.'

'Thanks again John,' she said.

He removed his hand from her cheek and straightened up. Now Joanna could see Alexander standing behind John with a look of fury on his face, which was immediately suppressed as soon as he realised she saw him.

'Hi Alex,' she said lightly. *How much had he heard*? she wondered.

'Oh, Alex, don't forget that the cue-to-cue is in forty-five minutes. Be there on time, there's a good boy,' John said. He walked past Alexander at the doorway and turned back to Joanna. 'As I said, love, the reward is much greater than the effort.'

'What the devil was he talking about?' Alexander asked, looking out the doorway at the tall figure.

'Nothing.' Joanna dismissed his question. He hadn't heard too much. *Just let him wonder,* she thought. 'What's up?' She assumed her professional manner.

'Not much, actually.'

'Sure, Alex, I really believe that.'

'Well, either nothings up or I've gotten used to the insanity around here.'

'Is it always this crazy close to opening night?' she asked genuinely interested.

Alexander settled himself in the other chair after removing a stack of file folders. 'I have never seen it this crazy, but then again, I've never acted here before. I think it's at least a little bit crazier than usual, because everybody knows how important the gala is to Upstage Theatre.

'Are you ready to go on? I understand that you've really picked up the part quickly,' she said. After seeing one rehearsal, she was interested in his point of view, especially since it would probably have a bearing on whether he decided to go to London.

'From past experience I can tell you that I never feel ready to go on. This time, absolutely not. Plus, there's some tension between John and me, for more than one reason. It's hard to take direction when you're used to being the director.'

What's the other reason? Joanna wondered. *Jealousy, maybe?* She liked that idea.

'But I don't have a whole lot of choice in the matter,' he said. 'I have to go on and I had to take the part in the first place - against my will as you well know.'

'We haven't talked much since then, Joanna,' he continued, his tone gentle but reproachful. 'Except about London and I'd rather not talk about that.'

'I know,' she said quietly. 'I'd rather not too.' She wanted to be angry, wanted some sort of violent emotion to allow her to keep her walls up against him. All she really felt like doing though, was throwing herself into his arms for the comfort she knew only he could give her – and that she hoped only she could give him.

'I miss you,' he said, his eyes nearly too intense for her to look at. 'I'll be so glad when this whole thing is over with and John goes back to the hole he slithered out of. Then we can get back to what we started four months ago.'

She remained silent. She didn't want to tell him that she was going on vacation immediately after the gala; she didn't want to be told his departure date, either.

'I guess we'll just have to wait to see what happens,' she said.

166

'Still no faith?' His face seemed to fall, seemed at once to be the face of Archie Rice, fifty years old, burned out.

Joanna shrugged and smiled sadly. What could she tell him? In the past two months all they had done was argue; she didn't enjoy that and it had damaged her. At times she wasn't sure what she was supposed to have faith in.

'Joanna, don't you know what that does to me, when you just look at me and shrug?' Alexander's frustration was evident. 'For the past two months you've either been so angry at me that you can't even speak to me civilly or you've been shrugging. I keep trying to get through to you and nothing works.'

He seemed to expect a response from her, but she didn't know what to say.

'How would you feel if you tried and tried to get through to me and all I did was shrug?' he asked.

'Listen, Alexander,' she said coldly, 'this is like the pot calling the kettle black. A couple of months ago, you treated the matter of our separation very casually. You let me go without a fight – in other words, you shrugged. So let's just be fair okay?'

'The only reason I was able to shrug at all, if that's what you think I did, was that I was scared of what we had, of all the love I had for you. I wasn't ready for it. But when I thought about it, I was more certain than scared that we'd make it. Does that make any sense? I didn't think we'd have any trouble working together. I didn't know at that point that I'd have to act and I didn't know that the Devil who's chasing you would offer me an audition with the National Theatre. But deep down, I was sure of you. I've been sure of you all along, but now I'm really starting to doubt. I don't know what to think.' Alexander ran his hands through his hair and looked at Joanna challengingly, eyes flashing.

'You're all strung out because of the performance, Alexander, so why don't we drop this conversation for the moment? We'll have plenty of time after the gala's over to see what happens. Don't worry about it for the time being. You can't waste the energy.'

Joanna felt deceitful, knowing very well that she'd be gone after the gala. The conversation might be put off indefinitely, but for now it was too much for her to deal with. He demanded honesty, something she was not brave enough to give.

'I don't consider this a waste of energy, Joanna.'

'All right, Alexander. I didn't mean it that way. I'm pooped. It hasn't been easy covering your work, putting in my work for the gala and keeping up my other accounts. That's all I'm saying. We're both tired and more emotional than we would be otherwise. For that reason – and because you have a cue-to-cue in ten minutes – I suggest we put this conversation off until later.'

'You're right – about the cue-to-cue. I've got to dash.' He rose from his chair and smiled; Joanna had the feeling that he was trying to reassure her that he was all right, that he was ashamed of his outburst, but his smile looked forced and pained.

'Have a good one,' she said softly.

'Wish me luck. This is going to be a long night.'

'I do. I'll leave the office door open.'

'Thanks,' He started towards the door, then stopped and turned to her again. 'I don't know why I'm saying this. I guess it's because I'm a glutton for punishment. I love you Joanna,' he said softly, appealingly.

'Good luck, Alexander.' *In everything,* she added to herself.

He seemed to sense her thoughts, for he lowered his head and shook it sadly. He walked out of the office and headed for the stage and the long, painstaking rehearsal during which each light cue would be coordinated with the actor's movements. Joanna heard a thump, as though Alexander had kicked the wall. Then she heard him say vehemently, 'Blast the theatre, blast William Shakespeare, and blast Joe for having been in that wreck!'

That Something Special

Chapter Fifteen

Joanna knew that the opening was sold out and that tickets were selling well for the other nights of the gala too. The afternoon of the opening, the board of directors had informed her at the final weekly meeting on the afternoon of the opening. Mr. Talman and Mr. Bradshaw had been ecstatic and had complimented her, thanking her more than once for her help. She was pleased, but at that point had been more interested in getting back to her condo for a bubble bath before the show.

She had bought herself what she considered a consolation prize; a blue-gray silk dress. Its lines were simple. The neckline was square and the waist was form-fitting with gathers that allowed the lovely material to fall gracefully around her long legs. She felt glamorous in it, and it helped boost her self-confidence. She felt that she could look every rich dowager straight in the eye and say, 'Yes, I did the publicity and the advertising for this gala. Isn't it wonderful?'

Joanna took her seat with the rest of the audience on Friday night for the opening of the gala. She looked briefly at the program, then at the crowd around her.

A large part of her concentration was back stage or in the dressing rooms – wherever Alexander was at that moment. She knew better than anyone seated in the audience about why he would be on stage that night. She was very proud of him even as she

171

begrudged him the circumstances. She had an irrational desire to grasp the arm of one of the dowagers and say, 'Yes, Alexander Carlson is just wonderful. Yes, I know him. We're very close. Of course, I'm awfully proud of him.'

She even found herself wanting to brag to someone - anyone, that he had been given the chance to audition for the National Theatre, the very same one that Laurence Olivier had helped create.

Her parents arrived. Her father looked tall and distinguished in a gray suit; her mother looked nearly girlish with her beautiful dress and shining green eyes. Joanna was glad they were there.

'Nervous?' her mother whispered, patting her arm.

Joanna nodded and continued scanning the crowd. She didn't feel talkative, a fact that her mother seemed to understand.

She spotted Bill and Sandy Jacobs in the crowd and waved; then saw Tom Dobson and his wife. Both Bill and Tom had been so helpful and supportive. In the two months since the board of directors had approved the gala, she felt she had learned a great deal about the theatre and advertising business. She now knew just how much work an artistic endeavour entailed.

She had also learned much about herself and how she functioned under stress. And she could not deny that she had learned a thing or two about love, about Alexander and about the problems one has to face in life. At that moment, nervous though she was, she felt that she could handle anything that might happen to her in the future, as though the Upstage Theatre experience had made her a stronger person.

The lights dimmed. The first segment on the program was the portion of *Don Juan in Hell* by George Bernard Shaw. When John came out onstage to say the words of the Shavian Devil, the audience applauded. Joanna was amazed as she saw still another side of the complex, infuriating man. He was completely believable as the dapper, wise and frightening Devil.

Next came the scene from Moliere's *The Misanthrope.* This was also skillfully acted. Joanna did not feel as personally close to it, since she was not well acquainted with any of the members of the cast; nevertheless, she felt proud of them when she heard the applause swell around her.

During the intermission, she led her parents to the lobby and introduced them to Bill and Sandy. Her father treated her to a glass of wine, which she accepted in hope that it would calm her nerves. She was growing more and more rattled as the time approached for the scene from *The Entertainer.*

'It's fantastic so far, Joanna,' Sandy said. 'You don't have to worry. Alexander will do fine. By the way, I heard advertisements for this gala on the radio every day. It was really plugged. Looks like it worked. Good job.'

'Thanks Sandy,' she said absently. 'Yes, I guess it's a full-house tonight and they tell me sales are good for the other nights too.'

'That's a feather in your cap, dear,' her father said, squeezing her shoulders.

The lights dimmed, indicating they had five minutes to get back to their seats before the next segment began.

As Joanna took her seat next to her parents, she wondered briefly if Alexander was suffering from stage fright. *It doesn't matter if he is. I'm nervous enough for both of us.* Her mother gave her hand a reassuring squeeze.

She realised soon enough that there had been no reason for her to be nervous. From the moment the scene started, she knew it would be fine. The electric rapport between the cast and the audience was nearly tangible.

When Alexander came on stage, Joanna barely recognised him. The expert theatrical makeup had dulled his richly coloured hair and added wrinkles to his face that the real Alexander would not have for another twenty years. It was uncanny, like looking into a crystal ball, as though Joanna had said, *Show me what my love will look like when we get older.* She had her answer now.

The character Archie was crude, thoughtless, dramatic and dissipated. Although it was impossible to like the character, it was also impossible not to admire the actor who evoked him so well that the audience pitied him. *It's incredible that Alexander first picked up the part less than a month ago,* Joanna mused. *He's a genius!*

She instinctively knew that Alexander was doing the speech his own way. There was a sincerity

174

to it that would not have been there had he taken John's direction.

The scene ended with Archie exiting while singing the blues. The applause was deafening. Joanna clapped her hands; hands that were cold from nerves and wonder. She clapped as hard as she could and when Alexander came on stage to take his bow, she clapped even harder. So did everyone else. The people around Joanna began to rise. Her parents did too. Alexander took a modest bow and acknowledged the rest of the cast. Joanna too was on her feet. Her mother elbowed her and Joanna grinned at her shakily as she felt a tear slip out of her eyes and down her cheek.

At last she understood the pull of the theatre. The actor not only needed attention, but also needed to give to the audience; needed to affect people so much that they'd want to rise up and give him a standing ovation.

That's how you'd know that you'd really shown them something they'd never seen before, she thought. Actors were not necessarily selfish; she knew that now, because Alexander had given so much to her and to the rest of the audience. The applause continued, and then slowly subsided and people returned to their seats.

Joanna might not have seen the segment from *A Midsummer Night's Dream* for all the attention she paid it. She was still wrapped up in *'The Entertainer,* shaking her head with pride and admiration. *He must go to London,* she realised. She believed strongly

175

that it was tragic and nearly criminal for a person not to develop his potential. He *must* develop his.

The audience applauded the Shakespeare's piece, but the overwhelming reception had definitely been for *The Entertainer*.

The full casts of all four segments came onstage and the audience rose in a single movement to give their second standing ovation of the evening. Hands joined, the actors walked to the front of the stage and bowed deeply. Alexander was in the centre; his eyes seemed to be scanning the audience. Somehow he found Joanna in the crowd and smiled broadly. In spite of the harsh stage lights, Joanna's eyes were locked with his, and she smiled in return – raising her hands above her head in victory applause.

The house lights came on and the audience went to the lobby to help themselves to fresh fruit, bread and cheese. Eventually, Joanna knew, the cast would come out to talk to the audience. Once everyone had gone, the opening-night party would start in one of the ballrooms of the Carlton Hotel. It would continue until the reviews came out in the Saturday-morning papers.

Bill and Sandy joined Joanna and her parents. Tom Dobson and his wife entered the group and were introduced to her parents.

'It was a smash,' Tom said enthusiastically. 'Joanna, you're a genius. So is Alexander. I have to give that guy credit for having learned the part so quickly. That he was able to play it so movingly is absolutely amazing.'

'See Jo, you didn't have anything to worry about,' Sandy said. She passed Joanna a slice of pineapple. 'Joanna was so nervous during the intermission.' She explained to Tom and his wife. 'I kept telling her that Alexander would do just fine.'

'He did better than I would have expected,' Bill commented. 'And John Hamilton was sure a spooky Devil in *Don Juan.* '

'Was I really?'

John had walked up behind Tom. He had changed out of his costume, but some vestiges of the thick makeup still remained and he looked a little paler than normal to the ghostly colouring.

'You were great John,' Joanna said. 'The whole thing went really well, didn't it?'

'It was wonderful,' the actor confirmed.

'And this must be Mr. and Mrs. Marsh. So very pleased to meet you,' he gushed, pumping her father's hand and giving her mother a kiss on the cheek.

'Uh, yes,' her mother said, looking ill-at-ease.

They continued their conversation, which they heard echoed by the little groups standing around the tables. How marvelous it was! Wasn't the Devil in *Don Juan* great? And wasn't that Alexander Carlson brilliant? It went on and on until Joanna doubted she could stand hearing Alexander's praises being sung any more.

Joanna's colleagues and her parents asked John several questions about theatre life. Then John turned to Joanna and said, 'Joanna, one night you

177

must watch the show from backstage. It is certainly different from being in the audience.'

'I'll have to do that,' she promised.

And then Alexander appeared. Joanna could feel her mother watching her and gauging her reaction. She introduced her parents to him; he shook hands with her father and said hello to her mother. Joanna didn't like the glint in her mother's eye, feeling that her mother might actually kick Alexander in the pants as she had threatened.

Luckily everyone began congratulating Alexander. John Hamilton mentioned the forth-coming trip to London. Alexander quickly looked at Joanna, but she fixed her attention upon her glass of white wine. Everyone asked questions about his plans until Joanna thought she might scream. Alexander had still not mentioned his departure date, which Joanna assumed would be while she was on vacation.

'Are you going to the party, Joanna?' he asked, for the first time directing his words to her.

'She's going with me, aren't you, pet?' John cooed. 'And you're taking dear little Rosemary, aren't you Alex?'

'I'm going to drive dear little Rosemary there, John, but her date is cute little Julian – you know, Puck in *A Midsummer Night's Dream.*'

'Then why don't you ride with us?' John asked.

Alexander glanced at Joanna and agreed. The two men settled on when and where to meet to drive to the hotel.

'Do you think you ought to go, Joanna?' her mother asked her quietly. 'You look tired. I can tell this is rough on you. It is on me too. If Alexander leaves you he is an idiot.'

Joanna shrugged, 'I don't really want to go to the party, especially not with the Devil over there. But I agreed and I don't see any way of getting out of it.'

'You can always leave early. There's nothing worse than being trapped into going to a party when you're not feeling festive at all.'

'Well, if they can get up on stage and act their little hearts out, I suppose I should be able to pretend that I'm having a good time.'

'Good luck.' Her mother replied giving Joanne a hug. 'And thanks for giving us the tickets to the gala – it was a night to remember.'

'Shall we go love?' John said boisterously. Joanna gritted her teeth and went.

The car resounded with Rosemary's babbling during the trip to the hotel. She was back to playing the overgrown cheerleader role and for some reason she turned the charm on Joanna.

'What a thrill it is to be an actress! Honestly, Joanna, I can't imagine that you'd ever want to go back to your office at Craft-Marker once the gala is over.'

'Rosemary, whether you can believe it or not, I'm moving back to Craft-Marker over the weekend.' Her head was starting to pound.

'Oh no! Well, we'll sure miss you. It's been great having you there to talk to, hasn't it, Alex?'

Alexander responded that it had been great having her at the theatre, but Joanna was sure that was just a polite answer.

The ballroom at the Carlton Hotel was jammed. A jazz band was playing loudly at one end; in front of the band people were dancing. Tables had been set up with more finger food and there was an open bar at the other end of the room. The crowd was comprised of cast, the crew, the board of directors, the financial backers and everyone's spouses, dates and family.

One wall was made up of glass doors overlooking the city. Outside some of them were small balconies where the brave could go to catch a breath of fresh air and enjoy the view from seven stories up.

Joanna excused herself as soon as possible and went to the restroom to comb her hair and take two aspirin. When she returned, she glanced around and saw Alexander surrounded by four women.

If I were in a better state of mind, she thought, *this would be very funny.* Just then Alexander caught her eye and threw her a look that said plainly, *Help! Save me!* Joanna couldn't help laughing.

She walked around the outside wall of the room, looking out the windows and decided to get some fresh air. It might help her headache. She opened one of the glass doors and stepped out onto the balcony, taking a breath of the cool night air.

'Joanna.'

She turned, startled. 'Oh, Alexander. You scared me.'

'Sorry.' He joined her on the balcony, taking a deep breath himself. 'It's nice out tonight, isn't it?'

'Yes.' Joanna felt slightly lulled by the traffic sounds and the breeze was indeed soothing. Her headache was no more than a twinge now.

Alexander leaned his elbows on the balcony railing and spoke without looking at her. 'Jo, we have to talk.'

'What about?' Joanna knew her tone of voice reflected her fatigue and she hoped Alexander would take pity on her and not press the issue.

'About my going to London. I'm not willing to drop the subject as easily as you might like/'

'Why not? What's the point?'

He sighed and shook his head. 'Joanna, I still haven't accepted the invitation to go to London. It's partly because I really don't care for the idea of becoming a full-time actor again. I took the part in *The Entertainer* only to save the show, so to speak. I had no intention of ever acting again. I think I told you from the start that the applause isn't worth all the pain and deceit involved. So although the offer's tempting, I do want you to know that I haven't decided yet. The other reason I've hesitated is that I don't want to hurt you.'

'Don't worry about me, Alexander,' Joanna said quietly. 'After seeing you perform tonight I'm the last person who would hold you back from using your talent. You were absolutely brilliant. I think you owe to yourself to go to the National and see what happens.'

'I can tell you what would probably happen. I'd audition, they'd accept me and then I'd spend the next five years playing trees and furniture and the third sword-carrier from the left. Nobody walks into a theatre and becomes a lead overnight. And if Mr. Hamilton thinks he has that much clout with the National, I think he's dreaming.' He admitted.

'Have the National people asked you to see them?'

'Yes, in fact they sent me an airline ticket to come for an interview with them.'

'Why don't you go and suss it out to see what they have to offer? They might have a part you'd like. You won't know unless you check it out and might always regret that you didn't follow-through with this chance.'

'But what about us?' he queried.

'We'll face that when it happens. The important thing right now is for you to finish up with the Upstage Theatre gala performances and go to the interview.'

'That's such a relief to me to hear you are on my side. I was thinking you were on the opposite side and would rebel against the whole idea.' He admitted.

Joanna smiled at him, 'I was a bitch for a while wasn't I, but I felt so deserted when you agreed to stay away from me for the two months.'

'So you really think I should go to London to see what they offer?' he said as he scratched his head.

'Yes, as I said, it's an offer you should not ignore. But I have one question for you. What if you decide you don't want to go to London – will the Upstage Theatre hold your position for you while you decide?'

He ran his hand through his hair, 'I really don't know what they would say.'

'Well the people who would decide that are in the room over there,' she said as she pointed towards the ballroom.

'I think I'll do just that. How about I meet you back here in say a half an hour?'

'I'll be here.' She replied with a smile. 'I hope they do keep that option open for you so you won't feel pressured to make a snap decision.'

He gave her a quick kiss and almost ran to the doors leading to the hall.

That Something Special

Chapter Sixteen

Alexander returned with a big smile on his face and was able to confirm that they would keep his job open for him.

'That's great Alexander. When are you supposed to go to London?'

'John has tentatively booked us on a flight leaving on January nineteenth.' He admitted.

'How ironic!' she said incredulously. 'I'm leaving for two week's holidays in Paris that day and I go via London. We will have to check to see if we would be on the same flight.'

'I didn't know you had planned a holiday?' he admitted.

'Well we weren't communicating enough to even discuss my life – our conversations always involved the theatre or your life there.'

'I have been very selfish haven't I? It really has been me, me, me hasn't it. I'm sorry for that but I was under so much stress I couldn't see what an ass I was being.'

'Well, we're over that now. What we need to do is get through the rest of the gala and check out things in London for you. And I will have a much-needed holiday in gay Parie!'

The next day, Joanna moved all her belongings out of the theatre and prepared herself to go back full-time to work with Craft-Marker on Monday. She still made an appearance at the theatre every day to check that everything was going well, but found everything was running like clockwork. On the Monday, she did run into John and asked him when he and Alexander were leaving for London.

'We're booked on British Airways flight BA369 leaving at 10:00 am on January nineteenth.' He replied. 'I understand you might be on the same flight?' he asked.

'Well that's good news, that's the flight I will be on too, but after I arrive in Heathrow, I will connect soon after with a flight to Paris.'

'I thought you were coming to be with Alexander.' He said with a hopeful look.

'No. I will be having a vacation for two weeks in Paris. I have to admit I am really looking forward to seeing Paris – I've never been there before.'

'So there's still hope for me after all?' he said in his booming voice.

'Afraid not – you and I are not a match.' She admitted, not wanting him to know that she would *never* be interested in him.

'Aw shucks,' he said with a hangdog look. 'Well, I guess I'd better get back to work – more rehearsals today.'

That night Joanna asked Alexander over for dinner and they discussed both their upcoming adventures.

'I spoke with John today,' Joanna began, 'and he says we are all on the same flight from Sydney to Heathrow Airport. I have to admit that when I told him I was going on to Paris, he thought he had a chance with me. I had to tell him that we were not a match. What I felt like telling him was that we weren't even close to being a match. I really don't like his flamboyant attitude towards women. He acts as if we will drop like flies in his lap. I think the fact that I was hard-to-get made him try even harder to make a conquest.'

'He's that way with his female co-actors as well, so I'm not surprised at your evaluation of him.'

'Have you heard anything more from the National in London?'

'Yes I did. I sent them a confirmation e-mail telling them that I would be coming and they have set up an interview with me for Wednesday January twenty-first.'

'Great. I'm glad you will have a bit of time to get over your jet lag. You will have to give me the name of your hotel and of course the e-mail address you will be using while you are there and I will do the same for you with mine in Paris.'

'That's great. I will take my tablet with me so I will be able to check my e-mails every day.' He said as he lovingly held her hand.

'I'm taking mine too, because my parents will be away caravanning with some friends while I'm gone. They have promised to send me pictures as they travel around Queensland and New South Wales.' Then she added, 'Are you nervous about your interview in London?'

'To be honest, yes I am. I find myself wavering between staying out of acting entirely and being ready to jump in with both feet. I'm going to ask them whether I can do any directing along with acting with them – leaving more doors open for me.'

'You've only got a few more performances as Archie. Are you going to miss that part?'

'Yes, in some ways I will because I put so much into learning the part in such a short time. Yes, I will miss Archie.' He admitted.

They enjoyed their dinner and Alexander the Great put on one of his shows of bounding from one end of the condo to the other – jumping on the sofa, the ottoman and even up into the bookcases, knocking over more books and did a finale by landing in Alexander's lap. He sat there very proud of himself while the two humans roared with laughter.

Joanna had taken Alexander the Great over to Bill's home with his food and bed and found herself tearful as she had a last cuddle with him. She had to deliver him the night before because they had to be at the airport at seven that morning and she wouldn't have had time to deliver him the day she left.

The morning of their departure, John and Alexander arrived by taxi, loaded her suitcase and carry-on in the boot and set off for the airport. Because the three of them would have taken up all the space in a normal taxi, they opted to hire a small van so there would be room for them and their luggage. John had brought quite a bit of luggage and because Alexander did not know how long he would be in London, he had packed an extra suitcase as well.'

They checked in and boarded the plane. They were flying business class and Alexander and Joanna had seats across from John.

'What kind of things have you planned while you're in Paris?' Alexander asked.

'Well, besides seeing the major ones such as the Eiffel Tower and the Arc de Triomphe, I'm hoping to see: The Louvre; Notre Dame de Paris; Champs Élyéés; Catacombs of Paris, Panthéon Paris and of course the Théâtre de la Ville.'

'Whew, and you expect to do that in two weeks?'

'Probably not, but I hope to see some of them.' She admitted. 'Have you been to London before?'

'Yes I have and loved it there. I have never seen such a well-run subway system anywhere. I was reluctant at first to try it thinking I would get lost, but found it a piece of cake. Originally I had fun taking the Black Cabs that are so old fashioned they are charming. And I visited quite a few of their theatres to catch their performances. Yes, London is a nice place.' He admitted.

It was a long flight, and Joanna was thankful that she was able to fall into a deep sleep. She had a couple of glasses of wine after dinner and fell fast asleep. Alex did too, but John had difficulties and was restless most of the trip. He was such a wound-up person that sitting for that long was agony.

He was able to keep himself busy by entertaining the flight attendants and was causing most of the first-class patrons to be almost rolling in their seats with laughter several times with his antics. Thankfully, he quieted down when it was sleep time, but was not able to sleep properly.

Their plane was a bit late and Joanna knew she would have to rush to make her connecting flight to Paris. Soon, almost too soon for Joanna, they arrived in Heathrow Airport and with the hustle and bustle of leaving the plane, Alexander and Joanna did not really have time to say a proper good-bye before she had to rush over to her next departure gate.

She settled into her seat feeling deserted. She was on her own again and she had to give herself a mental shake to remind her that she was now on holidays and was going to have fun even if it killed her.

Her hotel was a lovely one. As soon as she was settled, she visited the concierge and asked for brochures for the events she wanted to visit. She spent the rest of the day deciding where she wanted to go and making arrangements for tours to the events.

Far sooner than she expected, it was Thursday evening. She had spent a day sightseeing and was so tired she decided to order room service for dinner. She had just finished when the telephone rang. She knew it must be Alexander.

'Hello,' she said as she juggled the phone.

'Hello yourself,' said Alexander's baritone voice. 'How's gay old Parie?'

'It's great. I've spent the day sightseeing and am pooped. What's happening at your end?' Joanna realised she was holding her breath.

'It's going well. I had my interview with the decision-makers and with John's endorsement and the newspaper clippings about how well I handled things for the Upstage Theatre, they're thinking of offering me a fairly good part. They have to talk to the producers of the program before they make any commitment, so I won't know for a week whether it would be a good one or not.'

'What did they say about you producing some shows?'

'They said they would have to think about that and would have to speak with Upstage Theatre for some kind of opinion on my worth as a producer. So that too will take a bit of time. So at this point it is a wait and see thing.'

'Well, that will give you a chance to see more of London and possibly see some of their shows.'

'I've already got tickets for two of them. It will be great sitting in the audience instead of stressing over my performance or the performance of the actors I am responsible for.'

'Well that's great, Alexander,' she couldn't help but sigh knowing that this could separate them forever. But she did want him to succeed, so she brightened her voice to add, 'Be sure to phone me and tell me about the plays you see. I hope to see one here, but don't think it will be very effective for me because they will be speaking French.'

191

They discussed other matters and ended up the telephone conversation by telling each other that they loved one another and Alexander promised he would phone again soon.

Joanna sent an e-mail to her parents telling them the latest news and asked them how their trip was going. They replied with lots of detail about their adventures and enclosed many pictures of the sights they had seen. The couple with them seemed nice and they were having a wonderful time.

Every second day or so, Joanna sent her parents an e-mail telling them about her adventures in Paris and her parents did the same in theirs. One e-mail in particular intrigued Joanna and she couldn't wait to ask Alexander about it. She did not know the first names of his parents, but Joanna had told her parents that they were avid caravanners. Her parents had met a Julia and David Carlson that day and wondered if they could possibly be his parents.

Joanna quickly sent a red-flagged e-mail to Alexander asking him that question and within minutes he replied to say that indeed, those were his parents. What a small world it was, he wrote.

Joanna wrote right back to her parents giving them the news. Her parents immediately went over to their caravan and introduced themselves. They spent the evening together talking about what their children had been up to at the Upstage Theatre.

This again was relayed to Joanna and she sent the information to Alexander. He replied that he had just received an e-mail from his parents giving the same news.

Alexander promptly phoned Joanne, 'What a coincidence! Imagine our parents meeting each other by accident!'

'Yes, that is amazing.' She replied. She had really been missing him and sending e-mails did not fully fill the gap. 'It's wonderful to be talking to you again. Is everything going well in London?'

'Yes. It won't be long until I have my second meeting with the National. I will phone you that night to let you know what they say.'

'Good. I look forward to hearing from you.' She said, then added simply, 'I miss you.'

'I miss you too. What's going to happen to us?' he lamented.

'We'll face that when we know what our choices are. Be patient until you hear from the National. I love you.'

'Love you too. Bye for now.' She heard him blow a kiss to her as he hung up.

Joanna got up on Wednesday morning wondering how Alexander's meeting was going to go. Throughout the day she diverted her attention to doing more sightseeing, but made sure she was back in her hotel room by five o'clock so she would not miss him if he called.

When seven o'clock came and went, Joanna was starting to feel frantic. When the phone rang she jumped and grabbed it and it slipped out of her hand

and landed on the floor. She scrambled to retrieve it. 'Hello,' she said almost in a whisper.

'Are you there?' Alexander asked.

'Yes I am,' she replied with a bit more volume. 'Sorry, I dropped the phone.'

'Were you anxious to hear what happened?'

'Of course!' she said as the volume of her voice returned.

'Well, there have been some interesting developments. The part that was being offered to me is quite a good one from what I've seen of it. They have left me a script for me to examine. They also said they will let me produce the occasional play. So that was good news. However, just before my meeting with them I got a phone call from Upstage Theatre asking me whether I would consider doing the lead part in several productions they're considering for later on this year. They also agreed that if I wanted to, I could produce one or two plays.'

Joanna's heart skipped a beat – maybe he would not move to London after all and they could continue their courtship. 'So what are you going to do?' she asked.

'Well, the offer in London is for far more money and prestige that I could ever get in Sydney and the opportunity to produce a play of the caliber seen in London would certainly be more important and prestigious.'

'So what are you going to do?' she asked again with her heart in her mouth.

'I have asked both of them to give me a week to decide what I want to do.'

'I see.' She replied sadly – maybe she was losing him after all.

'So I have a week to decide and wonder if I can join you in Paris for your remaining days.'

Joanna would be returning to Sydney on Saturday afternoon. She realised how important a step this would be for them. They would be living together for those few days and that would make it even harder for her if he decided to stay in London. She explained this to him telling him that she didn't want any more hurt in her life.

'I can see it from your standpoint. So you don't want me to come to Paris?'

'I would like that very much, but I have been so hurt and I couldn't take any more hurt. If you decided to stay in London after we were together for those days I'd almost bleed with my anguish. I love you, don't you understand that?' she cried.

'I'm sorry. I shouldn't have asked you to do that. I will keep in touch with you and let you know what I decide to do.' He concluded his conversation with her.

Joanna cried for hours and did not have Alexander the Great to comfort her. She still had her support group though – her parents and wrote a long sad e-mail to them telling them of her anguish.

Never thinking they would do it, her parents immediately told Alexander's parents the situation their children were in. Alexander's parents then emailed their son admonishing him for dragging out his decision and hurting Joanna with his procrastination.

That same evening at eleven o'clock Joanna's phone rang. She wiped her tears and blew her nose before she answered, thinking it was her parents. It wasn't. It was a very angry Alexander.

'I just got off the phone with my parents who took a strip off me for 'dragging out my decision and hurting you with my procrastination' to use their terminology. How did they know what was going on between us?'

'I sent an e-mail to my parents telling them that I still did not know whether you were staying in London or not and how disappointed I was that things hadn't been decided. I feel like I'm on a tightrope hanging by a thread. I needed my support group – my parents, so told them what was happening.'

'Well, I'm ticked off that my parents have become involved.'

'That wasn't my fault. They're your parents.'

'As I said earlier tonight, I will let you know as soon as I decided which way I'm going.'

Chapter Seventeen

Joanna continued touring Paris, but her heart was not in it and she derived little pleasure seeing the sights. She was almost glad when Saturday morning arrived and she was able to go to the airport to go home. She wouldn't arrive until very late on Sunday night and Tom had told her to take Monday off seeing she had worked on the Saturday before she had left.

Bill picked her up at the airport as planned. They drove by his home and Bill quickly collected Alexander the Great, all his paraphernalia and new toys his children had given him.

'Was he a good boy?' Joanna asked.

'The best. My kids had so much fun with him. We were concerned when he sneaked out the door after the kids, but came right back when they came in. They are going to miss him.'

'I know I did. I could have done with a few cuddles during my holiday.'

'You don't look as rested as I expected. Didn't you enjoy Paris?'

'Paris wasn't the problem. Alexander was.'

'What did he do this time?'

'It's what he hasn't done that concerns me. He has been offered two excellent choices but he will be sitting on the fence for another week or so while he decides which choice he will take.'

'I don't want to pry, but can I ask what these choices are?' he asked as they drove close to her condo.

Joanna explained the two choices.

'Well, I can't say I blame him being tempted by the London offer. The National is a very prestigious theatre.'

'I know, but that means that our relationship would end with a bang. If he comes back here we would be able to continue and at least see where it would go.'

They pulled up in front of her condo. Bill patted her hand. 'I can see why you're upset. Hopefully he can make a decision before too long and get you off tender hooks.'

'I certainly hope so.' She said emphatically. 'And Bill, thanks again for taking such good care of my little man.'

'We all enjoyed having him.' he replied as he helped her take her luggage, Alexander the Great and his belongings into her condo.

'See you on Tuesday.' He said as he left.

Joanna cuddled Alexander the Great and gave him a treat. She found she was too tired even to unpack her suitcase. She crawled into her pajamas and was asleep almost before her head hit the pillow.

The next day she woke up feeling confused and it took her a few minutes to realise she was home again. Then her heart beat faster as she remembered her last talk with Alexander. He had not phoned her after his angry talk late Wednesday night.

She spent the day unpacking her suitcase, washing her clothes and playing with Alexander. The only time she left her condo was to stock up her fridge and grab a take-away dinner. As she watched

TV she could feel her eyes closing and gave in and went to bed much earlier than she would normally and woke up of course at five o'clock. *I might as well go into work early. I'm sure there will be lots of jobs waiting for me to do.*

She was the first one to the office and the janitor had to open the main door for her. 'Welcome back Miss Marsh.' He said. 'You're in early today.'

'Yes, I'm still jet lagged from Paris and woke up at five this morning.'

'Well don't work too hard.' He added as he went back to his task of cleaning one more office.

Later that morning, Bill waved as he passed her office and welcomed her back. Joanna was surprised by the number of people who did the same, welcoming her back to work. *It's nice to be wanted at work,* she thought.

She was just enjoying a cup of coffee at eight thirty when Tom phoned to welcome her back. 'Could you please come to my office? I have something to discuss with you.' He added.

'I'll be right there. Mind if I bring my coffee?'

'No bring it along. I'll get one too.'

After she entered his office he asked, 'And how was Paris?'

'It was great; I got to see many of their great tourist attractions. There were many more I would have liked to see, but ran out of time.'

'Did you hear from Alexander?'

Joanna filled him in on the developments.

'The reason I asked is that Mr. Bradshaw phoned me yesterday thinking you were back in the office to see if you could help him with something.'

'Oh no. I don't think I could spend another moment with that awful man.'

'In essence, what he wanted you to do was to contact Alexander and beg him to return to them. From what he said they will be very generous with him letting him act and direct as he pleases. Quite a turnaround from the past. They said the reviews in the newspapers resulted in the summer sessions being sold out and believe it was mainly because of Alexander's acting ability. Everyone says they want to see more of him.'

'I don't think I can do that for them. Alexander made it plain to me that he was going to make that decision on his own without interference from anyone. I don't even know what he's going to do.'

'Could you at least telephone Mr. Bradshaw and let him know where things stand?'

'Okay, but I sure don't want to have to deal with him in the future. If he wants more advertising, I'm hoping that Bill can do it, not me.'

'I can arrange that, but doubt if they will be happy.'

'Now, on a lighter note,' Tom added, 'I imagine by now you know we have hired a new staff member who was given your accounts to handle.'

'No, I hadn't. I was so busy trying to find the top of my desk under all the files there, that I didn't even have time to open the files of my regular clients.'

'Well, the reason we have done that is we have just received a huge new account that I want you to handle. It is with the Myer Department store. I would like you and Brian Marley to handle that account. It will be a full-on job. You will do the women's fashions and Brian will do the men's fashions. They will have other firms looking after children's clothing, pharmacy, hardware, toys etc. but we will have the adult clothing account.'

'Wonderful. Have you set up a meeting with them?'

'Yes, for Thursday, but in the meantime, I want you and Brian to get as much information as you can showing what advertising they are doing there. Do you think you will enjoy that account?'

'For sure. It will be great doing it.'

'It will also mean you will receive a raise because this is a much more important client who pays well.'

'Excellent. Maybe I'll be able to go back to Paris next year!'

'I'm sure you can.'

'Well, I'll pop into Brian's office and see if we can get busy with our new account.' She said as she left his office. 'By the way, thanks for the new account. I'll give it my best shot.'

He waved goodbye.

Brian was just as excited about his new account too and the two of them scoured the library, bought a copy of every newspaper they could and even checked with friends to confiscate any old papers they had to look at the past ads that had been used to advertise adult clothing.

'I wonder who had the account before us?' Joanna asked.

'It was the Baker Enfield Advertising firm. Two of their major advertising experts were in a fatal car accident and they don't have anyone with enough experience to take over the account. This is a great account for Tom to have obtained. I'm sure he worked hard getting it.'

'This is going to be fun, don't you think?' Joanna said with a smile.

'Oh yeah. When I told my wife about it, she was over the moon. Maybe I will earn enough now to buy the home of our dreams. Yes, I am very excited about this account and plan to give my all to the men's clothing advertising.'

'So am I – going to give my all to my own new project, that is.'

Joanna and Brian put in fourteen hour days for the next ten days, but Joanna was still aware that she was sitting on tender hooks as she waited to hear from Alexander. He hadn't phoned or sent an e-mail. She'd decided that she wouldn't contact him first. It was hard, really hard, but she kept herself so busy that she was able to divert her attention to her new account.

Friday afternoon, almost two weeks after she had arrived back, Joanna and Brian were working in the conference room sifting through the information they had accumulated about Myer advertising. They had realised that their individual offices were too small to accommodate the large amount of advertising material, so had asked permission to use the conference room.

They were presently working together to think of a new slogan for the most recent catalogue of men's and women's clothing.

'What do you think of this one?' Joanna asked Brian. She turned as she saw someone in the doorway and nearly fell off her chair when she saw that it was Alexander. She thought her heart was going to beat out of her chest. Was he here because he was going to stay or was he here to personally tell her he was going to take the job in London, so had just come to clear up things in Sydney.

Her hand went to her chest in shock. Alexander asked, 'Could we go to your office Joanna?'

'Sure. Brian, please continue to brainstorm. I'll be back as soon as I can.

When they got to her office, Alexander closed the door and went over to her and gave her a big hug. Joanna remained stiff, trying not to let herself feel how good it was to have him near her again.

'Why are you here?' she finally asked as she motioned him to a chair.

'I was going to phone you, but figured that I wanted to tell you my decision in person.'

'Well …?' she asked as she held her breath, not really feeling ready for his answer.

'After thinking it over carefully, I've decided to take the Upstage Theatre up on their offer. They got in touch with me again in London and pleaded their case. I will have lots of freedom to act and direct with them in an environment where I feel comfortable. So I'm staying in Sydney!'

'Why didn't you take the London job?' Joanna was stunned by his decision – she had seriously though he was out of her life for good, that the offer was so good he couldn't turn it down.

'It would have been a wonderful opportunity and I could have gone far with them, but then I thought of what I would be leaving behind.'

'And what was that specifically,' Joanna asked as she again held her breath.

'You of course. And Max. And my lovely home. So many things that I love that I didn't want to leave. I'm home to stay and I want you to be there with me. Am I too late to ask whether we can try again?'

'You know my answer to that! Of course I want to try again. This time though, I don't want the Upstage Theatre people to interfere at all. Bill will be looking after their account from now on. I have a new one that is fabulous.'

'You have my promise that they won't interfere again. I love you, I love you, I love you.' He added as he came around the desk to give her a huge hug and passionate kiss.

'Now, I'd better let you get back to work. I still have to collect Max at my neighbours and unpack.

Then I'm going to crash for the next sixteen hours – I'm beat.'

'You do that. Can we get together for dinner tomorrow - Saturday? I'd like to come to your place and can bring the fixings.'

'Sounds good to me. You might have to rouse me out of a deep sleep though and have a very groggy companion.'

'That's okay. Max can keep me company.'

That evening when Joanna went back to her condo she was so happy she scooped up Alexander the Great and danced around the room with him.

Her thoughts had changed so much in the few hours since she had seen Alexander that afternoon and she anticipated that they were over that rough patch in their relationship. *He really does have that something special* she thought as she sat stroking Alexander the Great.